SPICY BITES

MASKS

2019

ROMANCE
WRITERS
of Australia

Masks 2019: Spicy Bites Anthology

Anthology of Short Stories published by Romance Writers of Australia Inc © 2019

Print ISBN: 978-0-6485877-2-9

Ebook ISBN: 978-0-6485877-3-6

Spicy Bites Coordinator: Jayne Johnson

Cover design by Lana Pecherczyk

Edited by Libby M Iriks - Perfect Pear Editing

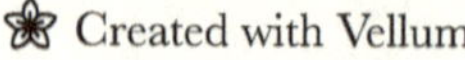 Created with Vellum

SPICY BITES

MASKS
Short Story Anthology
2019

Contents

Even without any erotic connotations, masks have so many different uses – to protect the face, to hide one's identity, to perform the part of someone else, to aid with sleeping, and to keep things hidden.

Masks can be physical or emotional. Many of us wear a mask at work that we strip away when the weekend comes around. Some of us wear a mask all the time so we don't have to continually explain away our hurt or pain.

A mask is a very personalised item – from guys in a welding shop who each have their own face mask adjusted to fit their own heads, through to the intricate, beautiful masks of the Japanese theatre style Noh, to individualised sleeping masks – think Holly Golightly in the movie Breakfast at Tiffanys with her turquoise mask, painted closed eyes with long golden eyelashes. Our masks can tell something about us.

Or, if we prefer, our masks can hide everything about us.

Adding in the erotic connotations, masks can be used

to increase pleasure, hide identity, fulfil a fantasy or indulge a fetish.

And on that note, I am pleased to present this year's edition of Spicy Bites – Masks. I hope you enjoy all the ways our authors have found to use the theme in their stories.

Regards
Bree Vreedenburgh
President 2018-

Welded to her Rules

MAISIE WHITFIELD

IVY MCCALLUM WAITED until his breathing was deep and even before she inched away, one millimetre at a time. The heavy canvas rustled as she folded it back, exposing their naked bodies to the moonlight.

He stirred, murmuring in his sleep.

Ivy froze, biting her lightly bruised bottom lip, and allowed herself one last glimpse. His charcoal eyelashes fluttered, and a smile flitted over his kiss-swollen lips.

No names, no strings, no regrets, she reminded herself, relieved when his handsome features relaxed back into slumber. The last thing she needed was those velvety brown eyes to flicker open and offer her the world.

Cold air caressed her skin as she shimmied over the tailgate of his F250 truck and tugged on her clothes. Her common sense may have taken a momentary nosedive, but at least she'd stuck to a few basic rules. Not the one about one-night stands obviously, nor her 'no sex on the first date' rule. Those had gone to hell when she'd taken his hand and led him away from the rodeo ring. Besides, the second rule only applied if she were planning on a second date. Which she most certainly wasn't. Lack of protection had been one of her deal-breakers, that and a refusal to share personal details. Which, when she thought about it, was just another form of protection, safeguarding her head and her heart.

Ivy weaved through the dark rows of utes and four-wheel drives. A few diehards still sat around campfires, so she kept her head low as she skirted around the campground, hoping she wouldn't recognise anyone, or worse, be recognised doing the walk of shame.

Magpies cleared their throats, readying themselves to begin their dawn chorus as she snuck out of the recreation reserve. By the time he woke up and realised she was gone, she'd be miles away.

DANE HENDERSON WOKE with a smile on his face. The night had gone beyond a quick favour manning the bar, but he certainly wasn't complaining. He'd been captivated by her from the minute he'd laid eyes on those long, glossy curls. She'd sat on the hay bales, watching the musicians instead of the bucking bulls. While the other women sat in clusters and couples, the onyx-haired beauty seemed content in her own company. He'd kept one eye on the customers as he served drinks and one eye on her, trying to figure her out. Was she waiting for a tardy boyfriend or a chatty friend who'd been sidetracked by one of the cowboys? From the look of those strong arms, she could be a barrel racer, or one of those brave new breed of cowgirls, breaking into the dangerous sport of rodeo riding. He'd been quick to serve her when she came up for another rum and coke and had somehow managed to make her laugh. Seeing her face light up with amusement was addictive—

he'd shamelessly summoned up his entire repertoire of bad jokes and then some until he'd finished his shift.

Dane yawned happily as he rolled onto his side. Just thinking about the taste of her made him hard again. He reached across, wanting to cup those sweet breasts in his hands and lose himself inside her once again. Disappointment washed through him when he discovered the other side of the swag empty. Dane blinked the sleep from his eyes. All that remained was a curly strand of ebony hair in the middle of the pillow. That and the glorious smell of her on his skin.

He sat up in the swag, swivelling to see the world beyond the back of his ute. The sky was painted a vibrant ochre and bottlebrush red, but the morning's beauty was tainted by her absence. He lay back on his elbows, reliving the memory of her writhing on top of him, as his trademark optimism found a positive spin for the situation.

Mightn't be a local yet, but it shouldn't take me too long to track her down and treat her the way she deserves.

IVY DANCED as her playlist rocked The Waifs. If she weren't already wearing her thick heat-proof gloves, she would push the volume higher.

She lifted her welding mask and viewed the perfect metal seam. Nearly done. Another welding rod and the bench would be as good as new. Ivy flicked her head, forcing the welding mask back into place, and tapped the handpiece against the steel. Sparks flew in the air, their blue, green and red glow visible from underneath her dark visor.

She lost herself in the music and the molten metal, her thoughts drifting to the man she'd met last night. He hadn't been intimidated by her muscles like some of the men she'd known. In fact, he'd complimented her physique as he helped her undress, running his lips along her stomach until he found another part of her body he liked just as much.

Ivy picked up the heavy bench with ease, her biceps flexing, and allowed herself a small smile. There had been something about his kind eyes and unflappable optimism that made her laugh, made her feel special. That and the fact he knew his way around a woman's body and took his time to pleasure her before he'd sought his own release. Perhaps it would've been nice to lay in his arms until the sun came up and wake him with the same passion she'd displayed under the cover of darkness.

Get real, Ivy, you know better than that.

Too many eyes watching.

She hurried to finish the welding repair, knowing she'd feel more confident about her decision when there was a thousand-kilometre buffer between her and temptation.

DANE DREW up alongside his cottage and gathered the wayward chicken from the front porch.

'You can't keep sneaking over in the middle of the night and expecting a four-course breakfast, Hetty. The new flock might follow suit, and then where will we be?'

He scooped up the old hen and smoothed her red feathers. She puffed herself out in protest as if reminding him that she knew he'd spent the night elsewhere. A tortoiseshell cat emerged from the hydrangea bush and followed them to the old chicken coop.

'You too, Tabitha. New chickens will be arriving any minute, and I'm relying on you to keep the mice away.

Two hundred chooks need plenty of grain. Can't afford a mouse plague.'

For the past six months, Dane's new venture had consumed his every thought. When he hadn't been renovating the ramshackle old cottage, he'd been contacting chicken breeders and building chook tractors in readiness for his free-range flock. And today, after years of planning, it would culminate with the delivery of his twelve-week-old birds and installation of his specially commissioned sign welcoming visitors to Snake Valley Free Range Chickens.

Dane whistled as he went about his morning chores and snatches of the night before flashed through his mind. What was it she'd whispered? Something about no names and no regrets? He looked out at the paddocks, his mind worlds away from farming. Instead, he was captivated by the memories from six hours earlier.

'Trust me,' she'd whispered, catching his earlobe with the tips of her teeth and pressing herself against him.

He'd groaned, grabbing her hips and angling her even closer. Their kisses had been gentle at first, then more frantic as she swept her tongue into his mouth and nipped at his bottom lip. She'd wanted more. He'd *needed* more. And if she'd run her hands up and down his fully clothed body once more, he would've exploded in his jeans.

'Shall we find somewhere more private?'

She'd nodded and grabbed his hand, pulling him towards the quiet rows of utes and four-wheel drives.

'Which one's yours?'

He'd led her to his vintage truck on the far edge of the car park. They'd worked well together, tugging the leather straps of his swag, equally impatient to get it unrolled. His zipper had bulged with anticipation, and he'd seen his own lust reflected in her dilated pupils. They'd undressed in the moonlight and made love under the khaki canvas.

A laughing kookaburra broke into his reverie.

Get a grip, Henderson. The chook delivery driver will think you're whacko if he arrives to find you staring into space with a hard-on.

Dane readjusted his jeans, walked across to the stock trough and splashed cold water on his face. For all her sex-appeal, she'd been wrong about one thing. He did have regrets—one, that he'd fallen asleep, and two, that he'd failed to notice her slip from his swag sometime between two a.m. and dawn.

Soon as the sign's up and the new chooks are settled, I'll get to work finding her.

IVY STEPPED out of the shower and wrapped a towel around her body, catching her phone just before it rang out.

'McCallum's Mobile Welding, Ivy speaking.'

'Darling, it's me. We're running late. Are you staying for dinner? Bob and Daisy are looking forward to seeing you too.'

Ivy laughed at her mother's lie and quickly gathered her belongings. Last time she'd checked, the private boarding school her stepsister attended was a solid three-hour drive away, but she couldn't be too careful.

'I'll see you next time I'm in town,' she said, knowing that her stepsister and stepfather wouldn't care whether it was in six weeks, six months or six years' time.

'We worry, darling. Perhaps if you just *tried* the real estate job? It'd pay better. And you wouldn't have to get so filthy every day.'

Ivy bid her well-meaning mother a hasty farewell. Why did her family find it so hard to accept she actually liked getting her hands dirty? It wasn't like she was the only female boilermaker in Australia. She doubted they'd even notice the bench she'd repaired, but she felt better knowing she'd worked for the hot shower and the free bed.

Not that I used it, she thought with a grin, rumpling the sheets so that it wasn't obvious she'd spent the night in the back of a stranger's ute.

She tugged on the same jeans she'd worn the previous evening. They hugged her butt in all the right places. Teamed with a few cans of Dutch courage, her outfit—so different to the baggy clothes she wore to work—had given her enough confidence to flirt with the tall, dark-haired barman.

He was different to the younger hoons who flogged their utes doing circle work, the tradies she usually hung out with, and the cocky young farmers who believed their privilege and family's wealth made them God's gift to women. And she'd liked his reaction when she'd told him the rules—as if he was genuinely disappointed he wouldn't get to know her.

No names, no strings, no regrets.

He'd hesitated when she'd said that, and for one long moment, she'd worried he was going to break the spell they'd woven. Ivy's body had trembled, pulsating with need as he pondered her request. She'd closed the gap between them quickly, the idea of not knowing which name to scream out when she came making it even hotter.

Ivy's memories of her brazen behaviour made her face burn. She looked into the foggy bathroom mirror, a smile tugging at the corner of her mouth. It had been a long time since she'd allowed herself to get close to someone. And a barman, of all people.

Biggest cliché in the book, Ivy. He probably chooses a new girl every weekend.

But as she gathered her belongings, she struggled to picture the handsome man as a serial Romeo.

Ivy tossed her backpack into her Ford Ranger. In four hours, she'd be in a different state, where no one knew her name or made demands on her life.

DANE LOOKED AT HIS WATCH. The welding guy still hadn't arrived. Normally, he'd let it slide, but the free-range egg certifier was due for the official inspection next week and he wanted to make a good first impression.

Might as well get the ball rolling, he thought. It'd be a damn sight more productive than standing around here fantasising about last night's mystery woman.

Dane slung a coil of rope over his shoulder and climbed the tall tree overhanging the entrance gates. He threw the rope around a large limb. At least by the time Kevin arrived with his welding gear, the new sign would be in perfect position arching over his driveway entry.

The view from the top of the red gum was spectacular. Green paddocks as far as the eye could see. Even the new chickens had settled in quickly, already fossicking for worms and exploring their new surrounds. He shimmied down the tree and attached the sign to the other end of the rope.

Gravel crunched under tyres in the distance, and Dane turned to see an unfamiliar ute negotiating the long, bumpy track. The dust trail cleared. Dane's curiosity piqued as he read the sign-writing underneath the dark tinted windows—McCallum's Mobile Welding.

What the ...?

Slowly, the window rolled down.

Dane did a double take, a smile spreading across his

face as he stared into the cobalt eyes that had captivated him last night. He hurried to lower the dangling sign to the ground.

'You're not Kevin. You're … you. I wasn't sure …' Dane shrugged his shoulders, trying but failing to keep the goofy smile from his face.

She's *come to find* me.

IVY'S MOUTH DROPPED OPEN. It was the sexy barman from last night.

She closed her eyes as she pulled the ute to a stop.

No. No. No. This is all wrong. But as much as she tried, she couldn't unsee the name or address scribbled on the notepad beside her. What use were the rules if she knew his name and where he lived? And, if the massive steel sign dangling from the red gum tree was any indication, she now knew he ran a free-range chicken farm on the outskirts of her hometown as well as tending rodeo bars.

And the signwriting on the side of my ute has completely annihilated my anonymity, too. Damn. This wasn't how today was supposed to go.

She wished she'd ignored her old boss's phone call half an hour ago. If she'd been another few kilometres north of town, she would've been out of range, the call would've gone straight to voicemail and then she wouldn't be standing in front of Dane.

This is where loyalty, sentimentality and rash decisions get you, Ivy. She cursed under her breath. It was hard to be cross at the handsome man standing there, positively delighted to see her. *God, did he have to be so damn sexy? This is going to be tough.*

Ivy fixed an aloof smile on her face, hoping it looked pleasant enough. Not eager. Not rude. Just pleasant.

She leaned out the window and his voice cut through the silence, penetrating the veneer she'd been carefully cultivating.

'It's you … I wasn't sure …'

She closed her eyes briefly, trying to remind herself of the rules. A hint of his scent wafted into the car—peppermint and campfire smoke, the combination suggesting he'd skipped the shower but remembered the toothpaste on his arrival home.

Just like ripping off a bandaid, she told herself, sweeping her feelings aside as she prepared to cut across his cheerful welcome.

'Kevin had a family emergency. Asked me to come out instead. I don't normally service this area, but …' She trailed off, annoyed at her steadily fading resolve.

No names, no strings, no regrets.

She took a deep breath and continued. 'Anyway, he sends his apologies. Guessing this is the sign you need welding in place? You want to hoist it up again while I get the welder sorted?'

Ivy saw the confusion in his eyes as she stepped out of the ute without waiting for an answer, and skirted around him to assemble her equipment. She felt like a prize bitch, but it was how it had to be. The quicker she finished the job, the quicker she could get out of there and get him off her mind.

She cranked up the generator, unlocked her toolbox and set up the welder. She could feel his gaze on her as she slipped a pair of overalls over the top of her jeans and shirt, the action feeling more intimate than undressing in front of him last night.

He spoke, his voice strained.

'Right … well.'

A rare twinge of regret settled in her stomach as she pulled out her welding mask. His reaction to seeing her—as if he thought she'd sought him out—would have made a weaker girl blush with joy. A tiny part of her wondered if maybe one day she'd ever let herself be that type of girl, but she chased the regret away.

Dammit, Ivy. Now two of your rules are shot to hell.

She twisted her hair into a plait and strode towards to the entrance gates, craving the shield of her welding mask. The less she looked at him, the easier it would be to walk away a second time.

DANE FELT like he'd been kicked in the nuts. It was her. There was no forgetting those bright blue eyes and that beautiful face. His cock responded like a homing pigeon coming in to land, remembering every inch of her luscious body and wanting more. She'd seemed so perfect last night. And now, after discovering she could hold her own in a male-dominated industry, he found her even more appealing. He wanted to pull her out of the ute and fuck her against the bull bar, but that was evidently the last thing on her mind. The way she'd shut him down as if last night had meant nothing to her … What was with that?

Where the hell's your pride, Henderson? It's pretty obvious you didn't rock her world quite the way you thought.

He worked quietly, checking the laser-cut sign was level before clamping it to the posts he'd cemented in place the previous week. She flicked the welding mask down with a swift nod of her head, preventing any further conversation.

He averted his eyes as colourful sparks flew from the equipment in her hand, doubt clouding his mind. It had been a long time, but he was pretty sure her crescendo of moans and gasps last night had been genuine. Maybe he'd made her come too fast, or not fast enough …? Maybe he should have offered an encore performance instead of falling asleep, completely sated?

Dane stuck his hands in his pockets and pushed his shoulders back as the final piece of puzzle floated into his head.

No strings.

He exhaled swiftly, relieved to have worked out the reason for her behaviour, but disappointed nevertheless.

They finished the job without talking, only the splattering of the welder and the hum of the generator cutting above the sound of calling birds. Living ten kilometres out of town, with no neighbours in sight and only the weather and wildlife to interrupt his train of thought was normally a good thing. But for the first time in a long time, as he helped her pack up her equipment, the property felt isolated and lonely.

Dane stretched out his hand.

'I'd offer you a coffee, but I can see you're itching to go,' he said ruefully. 'Safe travels, Ms McCallum.'

He wanted to invite her into the cottage for a hell of a lot more than coffee, but he clamped his lips shut and clung to the remains of his pride.

IT TOOK all of Ivy's resolve to open the door to her ute. She didn't often invite guys like Dane into her life, let alone her bed, and if she didn't act soon, her traitorous body would pull rank over her everlasting struggle for self-preservation.

You could be in his arms in just two steps. Pick up where you left off in less than a minute.

Instead, she murmured a quiet goodbye, fighting her own ambivalence. She lifted a dusty boot, about to pull herself up into the driver's seat, when he yelled out.

'Stop!'

The guy was optimistic, she'd give him that. Most men would have been happy to see the back of her after this morning's disappearing act and subsequent stand-offishness. Handsome, hot as hell, sensational in the sack and determined—he'd make someone a fantastic husband one day, she thought as she turned back to him. The stricken look on his face jerked her out of her funk.

'Seriously, stop! There's a snake in your car.'

She reacted as if he'd thrown a pot of boiling oil over her, launching herself away from the car and running in the opposite direction. If there was one thing she feared more than vulnerability, it was snakes. Big ones, little ones, fakes ones, pet ones—she hated every single one of them with all her might. Ivy's heart pounded in her chest as she steadied herself against the gate, clamping a hand over her mouth as Dane peered into the ute's footwell.

'Tell me you're joking?' Ivy's voice was meek.

He jerked back, shutting the door quickly.

'Wouldn't joke about a tiger snake. It's not a happy camper, either. There's a good snake catcher in town, I've had him here a few times this month already. Come to the cottage and we'll call him.'

She stayed rooted to the spot, her eyes glued to her ute.

He spoke again, a hint of amusement in his voice. 'Or you can wait here and I'll call him for you?'

Ivy shook her head vehemently, her skin crawling at the thought. She jogged across to him, overwhelmingly eager to follow him up the driveway.

DANE GRINNED as he boiled the kettle, wondering how such a tough woman—who clearly fought tooth and nail to maintain her independence—could be so petrified of a three-foot-long reptile. Sure, they were deadly as sin, but part and parcel of life in a rural area.

He turned back to the dining table, captivated by the sight of her stepping from her overalls.

She caught his gaze and smiled bashfully. Their hands met as he passed her the cup of tea, their movements stilted as if they hadn't had mind-blowing sex less than twenty-four hours ago.

'Thank you for spotting the snake. And for putting up with my bad attitude this morning. You didn't deserve … I'm not … I don't usually …'

Obviously, she was unused to apologising.

'My name's Ivy, by the way. Ivy McCallum, nomadic mobile welder and snake-phobic.'

He accepted the hand she stuck out and waved away her apology.

'Nice to officially meet you, Ivy. Sorry, but the snake guy's going to take a while. He's a popular bloke in these parts. There's a good reason this town was named Snake Valley.'

Her smile transformed her face.

God, she's beautiful.

Dane tried to conjure up another string of light-hearted jokes like he had last night, but his mind had gone blank. He stood up and moved across to the sink, looking out the window and focusing on the red hen pacing the chicken-wire perimeter of her coop, evidently determined to break out again. Ivy came to stand beside him, following his gaze.

Hetty wriggled through a gap in the wire and strode across the yard. She clucked triumphantly at them, preening her feathers as she settled on the verandah step.

'Does she escape often?'

'At least a few times a day. Early in the morning usually, when she can smell the toast cooking. She's a lady who knows what she wants.'

Ivy sighed so quietly he almost didn't hear it. She leaned towards him. He felt the heat of her body and steeled himself against gravitating closer.

Even her hair smells good, he thought, catching the shampooed scent of her glossy black locks.

Her eyes remained on Hetty. 'Doesn't she worry about getting gobbled up by a fox every time she leaves her pen?'

'I reckon a fox would come off second best against Hetty. Sometimes I share my vegemite toast with her. Can't help but admire the tough old bird.'

HIS WORDS FRAYED the final strands of Ivy's resolve. All the rules were broken now. She let her hand fall from the bench, so it rested against his thigh.

'Even though she isn't good at following the rules?'

'Yep.'

She ran her short fingernails along the seam of his denim jeans, listening to the way his breath quickened as she moved higher. When he didn't step away, she grew bolder, slipping her hand between him and the benchtop, her palm cupping his straining zipper. He was rock hard, just like he'd been last night when he slid into her.

God, she wanted him.

Heat spread through her loins as she felt how hard

she'd made him. She wriggled her hand, pressing, massaging and stroking through the thick denim.

He groaned and tugged her hand away.

'You're killing me, Ivy. I know this is what I want, but are you sure it's what *you* want?'

She shimmied sideways, wedging herself between Dane and the bench, and tilted her chin to meet his eyes. His hardness against her throbbing loins was delicious.

She spoke, her voice husky. 'Sometimes I'm too stubborn to work things out the easy way. Maybe I should take a leaf out of Hetty's book and be brave enough to go for what I want.'

He swept the hair from her face, leaning down to press his mouth to hers. The kiss sent shockwaves through her body, confirming what she'd known all along but had been too pig-headed to admit.

Her lips tingled. Her body burned with desire. She could feel herself growing moist 'And is this what you want?'

She nodded. 'Definitely.'

Her fingers trembled as she unbuttoned her top and pulled the fabric away from her shoulders, exposing a lacy pink bra. He dipped his head and used his teeth to drag the lace away, releasing her nipples, one by one. It was her turn to groan as she ran her fingers through his short hair, pressing him closer to her breasts. He captured a nipple between his lips, sucking it gently as he cupped her other breast.

Ivy wrestled with the top button of his jeans and he let out an appreciative growl as she squeezed the length of him. His mouth returned to hers, more urgent now as his hand skimmed her waistline and slipped inside her pants. She arched into his touch as he unzipped them.

Dane pulled his shirt over his head and Ivy admired

him in all his naked glory. He was just as fine in the pure daylight as he had been last night, illuminated only by the moon. She looked up at him coyly. His wolfish smile and dark chocolate eyes smouldered with lust.

This was a good idea. A really good idea.

The kitchen floorboards were soon covered in clothes. She smiled, licking her fingers one by one before reaching for him. He rocked his hips as she slid her slippery hands back and forth over his velvety length. He leaned against the kitchen bench, perspiration beading on his body as she increased her pace, only slowing when the silkiness on her hands evaporated. She pulled away with a wicked grin. Dane had put her first last night—it was time to return the favour. She knelt and took him in her mouth, sucking hard. She heard his breath quicken and took him deeper until he gently pushed her shoulders away and pulled his hips back. He placed a hand on either side of her face, lifting her chin until she met his heady gaze. His voice was deep with arousal, the timbre of it turning her on even more.

'Tell me where you want me, Ivy.'

She rose up on tiptoe and whispered into his ear.

'Inside me. All over me. Now.'

* * *

THE FLOORBOARDS CREAKED as he carried her to his room. Privacy and daylight were luxuries they hadn't had last night, and the sight of her in only a thin layer of pink lace made him harder still.

Sexy as fuck.

He lowered her to the bed and peeled off the last of their clothing. Forcing himself to take it slow, he kissed his way down her torso and threaded his fingers through her silky triangle of black curls. He dipped between her soft folds. She was hot. Moist. Ready. A groan ripped through the still air, but he couldn't tell whether the sound of exquisite pleasure had come from her mouth or his.

Ivy arched her back and he watched her watching him, her eyes heavy with desire.

'You're making me so hot.'

Dane's smile widened and he nodded.

'That's what I'm aiming for,' he said, ducking his head and tasting her.

She was sweet, slick and musky, just like last night. His arousal dug into the mattress, growing harder each time she quivered beneath his touch. He licked, kissed and caressed her to the edge of pleasure. She moaned and bucked beneath his mouth, digging her fingernails into his shoulders with each shudder.

He pulled a foil packet from his bedside drawer.

Ivy pushed him onto the bed and rolled the condom onto him before straddling his hips. She rocked faster. His blood pounded. Waves of pleasure built as he thrust into her. She bit her bottom lip, staring him straight in the eye as their climaxes ripped through their bodies.

No masks. No rules. Only unabridged pleasure.

Behind the Mask

CASSIE LAELYN

Ivy

'Get your butt out that door,' Kat commanded from underneath a plush doona.

'No, I'm staying,' I replied. If I went ahead with a snowboarding session while my best friend lay in bed nursing an epic hangover, I'd feel like crap.

Kat narrowed her eyes and the look, coupled with a damp washer draped over her forehead, made me want to laugh.

'Ivy Cooper, take off your serious mask for once. We're meant to be celebrating your twenty-fifth birthday. Go out and have fun. I'm a little hungover …' She winced and her skin blanched. 'Okay, I'm really hungover, but I'm not going to die.'

I pursed my lips. One thing I knew about Kat? She wouldn't give up until I was out that door. After a stare-off, I sighed.

'Fine. I'll go. But make sure you text me if you need anything.'

Her pale face brightened a notch. 'Deal. And make

sure you text me if the instructor's a hottie. Now go, you're already late.'

I grabbed my ski jacket, goggles and beanie.

'Okay, I'm going.' I laughed, heading out of our hotel room, and shut the door behind me.

Halfway down the stairs, I glanced at my watch. Shit! If I didn't hurry, the instructor would think I was a no-show. I jogged the rest of the way down the stairs and bolted across the main foyer, weaving around a mass of tourists wearing bulky ski jackets.

I shoved open the rear glass door, swung right and slammed straight into a rock-hard body.

'Sorry …' My words caught as I glanced up at the hunk of steel I'd collided with.

Oh, crap. Those impossibly bright blue eyes didn't belong to just any well-built dude. They belonged to the one and only Liam Cole—the guy I'd avoided for nearly two years.

He lowered his black ski mask, revealing a wolfish grin. 'Hey there, Ivy.'

I cleared my throat and retreated a step. 'Ah … hi, Liam.'

I peered around the deck, looking for a guy who resembled a snowboard instructor. Anything to avoid eye contact with Liam. 'I'm sorry, but I'm late for a snowboarding session.'

'Is that so?'

A hint of curiosity in Liam's tone made me glance at him. Big mistake. His grin curved into a full-blown smile, revealing a deep dimple on one side, accentuated by the dark stubble dusted over his jaw. My heart fluttered, heat spreading through my veins. That damn dimple got me every time.

Jesus. This was exactly why I needed to avoid him.

I stepped back, away from his hotness. 'Yep. So, I'll see you later.' *Or not.*

When I turned to leave, I spotted the ski lodge's logo on his jacket. *Shit.*

'Actually, I'm looking for someone who's late for a snowboarding session.'

My heart sank all the way to my fur-lined boots. *Please no.*

Liam glanced at the mobile in his hand. 'But … it's not you.'

Relief burst inside me like an explosion of confetti.

'I'm looking for Kat O'Brien. She booked two spots.'

Damn Kat! I bet she planned this whole thing. I should never have told her about Liam.

Before responding, I considered my options. I could lie, tell Liam I had no idea who Kat O'Brien was, and be on my way. Continue avoiding him until I died of old age. The idea appealed so bad. But later, the pain inside my chest would rocket to a whole new level.

I peered up at Liam and those ice-blue eyes sucked me all the way in. My breath quickened.

'That's me,' I murmured.

Liam's brows knitted.

'Kat's sick, so …' I shrugged one shoulder. 'It's just me.'

A wicked spark lit in his eyes and it set my damn panties on fire.

He smirked. 'What are the chances?'

I didn't even want to consider that. We'd had so many chances I'd lost count—and I'd blown every single one of them. 'Let's just get this over with.'

Liam laughed, deep and throaty. 'It's not like you to rush things.'

And there he went, throwing it in my face. But today, I

wouldn't bite no matter how much I wanted to. Because lowering the mask I'd forced into place meant acknowledging my true feelings for him. Feelings I'd buried so deep I had no idea how to unpack them.

I lifted my chin. 'Do I need to go somewhere to hire a board or do you have one?'

His eyes sharpened, studying me. My entire body sizzled under his stare, every nerve ending zapping with electricity.

'I've taken care of it, Ivy.' He motioned to the other side of the deck where a few boards stood upright in racks.

'Great,' I said, not bothering to simmer the sarcasm. 'Let's go then.'

After grabbing a board, I followed Liam to the chairlift.

My body jolted when the chair slammed into the back of my knees and I flopped down, almost losing my board in the process. Liam shot forward, catching my goggles as they flung off my head. He placed them in my lap.

I swallowed. His hand on my upper thigh made my stomach do flips.

His hand lingered for a moment, then he pulled away and relaxed in the chair, peering towards the snow-covered mountains.

'I'm going to take you to the back country. I know you can snowboard, so there's no fun in staying on the main runs.' He glanced across his shoulder and winked. 'Let's do something adventurous.'

The last time Liam suggested something adventurous, I freaked out and left town.

With my gloved hand, I clenched the metal rail of the chair and peered over the side. Would it hurt jumping from this height? Would the powdery snow brace my fall?

No, Ivy. You can do this.

My gaze drifted to the dark grey clouds building above. 'Should we ski far from the main lodge in this weather?'

As the words fell from my mouth, tiny, delicate snowflakes fluttered down from the sky. I watched, mesmerised as a few landed on Liam's charcoal beanie. The urge to rip it off and rake my fingers through his unruly jet-black hair surged through me. Tingles bloomed between my legs when I imagined him moaning as I scraped my nails along his scalp.

Heat flamed in my cheeks.

Liam twisted to face me, brushing the back of his gloved hand along my jaw. 'I'll protect you, Ivy. I always will.'

I turned away, not wanting to acknowledge the reason for the sudden tightness in my chest. Having a watchdog was one thing. But a lover too? No, I wouldn't think of that right now. I couldn't.

'Okay, get ready,' Liam said, his voice playful.

I thanked all the gods above when the turnaround point for the chairlift came into view. Another minute next to Liam and I'd surely combust.

I wiggled closer to the edge and clipped my boots into the board. This is where I screwed up every single time, either tangling my arms and legs or sliding off too late and landing flat on my arse.

Liam took my hand in his, sending a flash of heat through my veins. My heart twisted.

'I've got you,' he murmured. 'Three … two … one … go!'

With my free hand, I pushed off the chair the moment my board hit the snow. My legs wobbled, swaying back and forth and I flailed my arms trying to keep balance. Just as I was about to fall, strong arms snaked around my middle, holding me upright.

I breathed a sigh of relief but instantly regretted it. Liam's rugged earth-and-pine-needles scent, mixed with the crisp, fresh snow made my freaking toes curl.

I slid forward out of Liam's embrace and turned to face him. 'Thanks.'

This was a bad idea. I should've lied back at the lodge, returned inside to the lobby or gone straight to the bar. Having him this close, feeling the heat of his body next to mine, brought back too many memories. Memories I'd locked away tight.

I shouldn't give Liam the false hope of forever.

I shouldn't give *myself* the false hope we'd work.

* * *

Liam

Thirty minutes later, Ivy disappeared. *Goddamn it.* Just when I thought I had her back in my life, I lost her again. This time I blamed the bloody weather not my dumbass timing.

I twisted the board and skidded to a halt. The snow fell thick and fast, and I wiped the slush from my goggles, peering around to search for her. All I saw was white. Nothing but fucking white. Lifting my nose in the air, I tried to locate her position, sifting through the scents, searching for that hint of stormy rain. Which was near impossible considering the blizzard happening around me.

I spun to the left, catching Ivy's faint scent and took off towards it.

She had the world's worse sense of direction; I shouldn't have let her lead the way. A lump tightened in the back of my throat. What if I didn't find her in time?

As the thought formed, an aqua ski jacket came into view through the whiteness and I exhaled a shaky breath. A second later, I skidded to a halt in front of her.

'The weather's turning fast,' I shouted above the wind.

'No shit!'

'We need to find somewhere to wait out the storm.' I lifted my nose in the air once more and caught the rich smell of timber. Shelter was close by. 'There's a halfway hut not too far from here. We'll go there.'

'Are you freaking kidding me?'

There was no time to argue, I had to get her to safety. 'Ivy, it's too dangerous for you to be out in this weather and we're too far from the lodge to go back.'

Her pretty lips set in a hard line and I imagined her rolling her eyes at me from behind those goggles. 'You sure this wasn't your plan all along?'

I scoffed. 'I wish I could take the credit'—I opened my arms wide—'but we can stand out here instead if you'd prefer to die in the snow?'

She threw her arms up. 'Fine. Where's the hut?'

I pointed to the right even though she wouldn't be able to see it. 'Over there. I'll lead, but Ivy …' I leaned in, pointing to the ground beside me, 'I want you glued to me.'

When she nodded, I took off, keeping a steady pace so she stayed close.

By the time the hut came into view, Ivy's face was pale and her nose looked like it would snap if I touched it. Goddamn it. I should've given her my ski mask. I clipped out of my board and ushered Ivy inside, taking her gear and placing it by the door with mine.

The timber hut wasn't much, but at this point, I didn't give a shit as long as it sheltered her from the bitter wind. Built for emergencies such as these, I knew it would be unlocked and stocked with firewood and basic canned food.

Slipping off my beanie, I headed to the hearth and started a fire. In no time, heat filled the space. I stared into the flickering flames, unable to move as the gravity of the situation hit me—Ivy and I were alone together for the first time since … well, since I asked her to be mine forever.

Turning around, I found Ivy hesitating just inside the door. Light flickered over her beautiful features, sparkling like glittery stars in her bright hazel eyes. When her gaze locked with mine, I caught a sense of … longing. My chest squeezed. Would she finally say yes?

I padded towards her. I couldn't breathe, not this close. Not when I'd imagined this moment a thousand times, only to have it disappear.

This could be my last chance.

I tugged the zip on her jacket, pulling her closer. She sucked in a sharp breath. With slow and steady movements so I didn't spook her, I inched down the zipper before sliding the jacket off her slender shoulders. I'd missed her so much the pain was a constant ache inside my chest.

I couldn't let her slip away again.

I smoothed my palms over her warming cheeks, sliding them up to remove her beanie, discarding it on the floor. Loose strands of golden hair fell across her face and I swept the locks away, tucking them behind her ear.

Holding her gaze, I removed my jacket with the same unhurried movements and tossed it over the edge of the couch.

When her eyes dipped to my lips, my cock roared to life. I clamped my molars together to halt the wicked images forming in my head. It failed.

Unable to stop, I lowered my lips to her ear, inhaling her delicious scent. 'Come stand by the fire.'

'Okay,' she replied, a little breathless.

Finally, I had her within reach and there was nowhere for her to run. I wanted to remind her of us, of what we could be if she only gave us a chance.

I stiffened as my insides quaked with tremors, an unwelcome but familiar sensation. I wasn't the only one who wanted to see her, but I wasn't ready to share. No. Not yet. My fists clenched as my stomach twisted. I had to step outside and calm the hell down, otherwise I'd lose control.

I straightened. 'I'm gonna call in our location.'

Her brows lifted and fell. 'So someone rescues us?'

'No.' My voice deepened and I pushed down another tremor. 'So they don't.'

She glared at me with all the ferociousness of a tiger. A cute, adorable tiger.

I held up a palm, stifling a laugh. 'Before you jump to conclusions, there's no point in risking lives when you don't need rescuing. I'll take you back when the storm passes.' I brushed my knuckles along her jaw. 'You're safe with me, Ivy. You always will be.'

One day she'd get that.

I'd protected Ivy since her family moved to town when she was ten years old. I beat up that asshole Donohue for calling her fat when she was twelve. I kept her safe when she was sixteen and I carried her home from a party after her first failed experience with alcohol.

I excelled at keeping Ivy Morgan safe.

If only she'd trust me with her heart.

'Stay,' I pleaded.

Moments passed as I waited for her answer. If Ivy wanted me to send for help, I would. I wouldn't force her to stay.

Instead, she nodded and my heart all but exploded.

Without saying another word, I brushed a thumb over her bottom lip before walking out the door, closing it softly behind me.

* * *

Ivy

Howling wind skated across the roof of the hut while I paced back and forth, waiting for Liam to return. What was taking him so long?

Scratching sounded from outside. I stilled, sucking in a sharp breath, cocking my ear towards the door, trying to place the noise. The sound continued, followed by soft, faint whimpers. The moment recognition sparked in my mind, a smile warmed my face.

Crossing the room, I creaked open the door to find a large wolf with a long narrow jaw standing on the other side, its thick, glossy black fur dusted in snow. My heart rate steadied the moment my gaze landed on the wolf's eyes. I'd never forget the first time I saw those eyes, staring back at me from the forest behind my house on the night my family moved in. The same eyes that comforted me from the foot of my bed for over a week when my parents died.

The same pools of glacier-blue that drew me in less than an hour ago.

Liam's eyes.

I gathered the clothes scattered by the door and patted my leg for the wolf to follow me inside. He trotted in, circling the hut before returning to me. I crouched, scratching behind his ears as he licked my face, his tail wagging back and forth.

'Hello, gorgeous boy. I've missed you.'

The pang in my chest intensified. Until now, I hadn't realised how much I missed Liam, in human *and* wolf form.

The wolf puffed out warm breaths as I raked my fingers through its thick, furry coat, shaking off the snow.

As much as I wanted to spend time with him, I couldn't prolong my conversation with Liam any longer. It wasn't fair to keep him hanging on.

I cradled the wolf's snout between my hands. 'I'm sorry, boy, I know you want to protect me from the storm, but I need you to shift back.'

The wolf whined, licking the inside of my palm.

'I'm sorry, but I need to talk to him.' I stood, taking a step back. Summoning the command Liam once told me, I looked directly into those familiar blue eyes. '*Shift.*'

In one swift movement, the gorgeous wolf transformed back into Liam. He stood, towering over me in all his nakedness. Usually, I diverted my eyes, but this time, I couldn't turn away.

I'd fantasised about this moment countless times. Imagined kissing his golden-tanned skin or watching the fire ignite in his eyes when he claimed me as his. But, I always resisted. Because sex with Liam meant forever, and that scared the hell out of me.

But this time felt different, like I saw Liam through a different lens. For the past fifteen years, I'd masked my feelings for him. Now, stranded in a hut after two years apart, that mask threatened to slip free.

'Liam,' I breathed.

Liam's wild eyes darkened, resembling a dark, stormy ocean.

My gaze yearned to explore his strong, glorious body. I wanted to touch him, graze my nails over his firm pecs, down the ridge of his chest. I wanted to rub my thumb over the head of his swelling erection, long and thick and impossible to ignore.

Liam inched closer.

My heart pounded so loud it drowned out the wind swirling outside the hut.

He smoothed his knuckles along my jaw. 'My wolf missed you.' He paused. '*I've* missed you.'

He closed in until only a sliver of space remained

between us. The air thickened, and I struggled to rip myself free from the spell.

'When I asked you to be mine'—his palm trailed a path down between my breasts, halting at the hem of my pants—'you said you needed time.' His finger slid behind the waistband. 'Do you need more?'

Yes. No. I had no freaking clue.

His rough hands crept under the hem of my knit causing every ounce of air to escape my lungs in one swift *whoosh*.

'Liam,' I murmured, my breath quickening.

God, what was wrong with me? With a single touch, he turned my insides to molten lava and reduced my ability to form a coherent sentence.

'I've waited two years for you to come home, Ivy.' His hands slid to my hips. 'Two fucking years. And every single day, all I wanted to do was track you down, throw you over my shoulder and make you mine. But I let you go, gave you the time and space you wanted.' His thumbs made small circles on my hips, sending swells of pleasure between my legs. 'The time for running is over, Ivy.'

I'd tried to forget him, tried to let him go, but deep down, part of me longed for him to find me.

Liam lifted my shirt up and over my head, tossing it to the floor.

Oh, God. I couldn't make sense of the emotions flooding my body. Fear. Anticipation. A whole lot of freaking desire.

'How can you still want me when all I've done is push you away?'

His expression softened, and that wolfish grin returned. 'I've wanted you since I was fifteen years old. Hell, probably before that.' His fingers grazed up and down my sides. 'It's always been you and me.'

My heart skipped wildly in my chest. 'But … I'm not a shifter like you.'

Liam hovered so close to my lips I hungered for a taste. 'I love you for who you are. I always will.' He cradled my jaw between his hands. 'Kiss me, Ivy.'

The part of me I'd ignored for so long roared to life. A want, a *need* for Liam I'd always possessed. A yearning for this moment. A yearning for him.

I closed the distance and took his mouth with mine. A bolt of pleasure shot through my middle the instant our lips touched. Pure, white-hot pleasure. His lips warm and rough against mine, delivering the sweetest, most gentle kiss I'd ever experienced.

Liam tasted of wild, rugged earth. Of familiarity and comfort.

Liam tasted of *home*.

He was right. For as long as I could remember, it had always been the two of us. The moment realisation hit, I let go. I let go of my fears and opened my heart to him. I tore off the mask I'd held in place, that kept my feelings for him hidden.

Liam must've sensed the moment I surrendered because he tilted my head, deepening our kiss as he backed me against the wall. His tongue swept over mine causing a blaze of fire to rip through me, awakening my body, centring between my legs. My hands flattened against his hard chest, feeling a deep satisfaction rumble inside him.

Touching his strong muscles, his smooth, firm skin, made me burn all over.

With one hand, he cupped my breast, rubbing his thumb over the lacy fabric of my bra, causing my nipples to harden.

Liam drew back, his gaze locking with mine. 'Is this

okay?' He teased the bud between his fingers, sending waves of moisture to my core.

'Yes,' I breathed, dizzy with pleasure.

His cocky grin returned before he flipped down the bra and lowered his head, circling his tongue around the hard tip.

'God, Liam,' I moaned, shoving my fingers through his thick hair.

He sucked the nipple, flicking it with his tongue. 'Baby, I've wanted to hear that moan for so fucking long.'

Liam's hand travelled to the waistband of my pants, popped open the button and slid down the zipper.

Sweet Jesus. I swear I saw stars the moment his fingers brushed over my panties.

Turning his attention to my other breast, Liam stroked along the outside of my panties at a slow, tortuous pace. Fire coursed through every single cell in my body. A coil of tension tightening low in my belly with each brush of his finger, needy for release—

He withdrew his fingers, making me gasp from the sudden loss of contact.

Liam straightened; his wild gaze held mine. 'I want you, Ivy. I want to slide my cock deep inside you.' He took my mouth in a hard, rough kiss. 'Tell me you want this.'

My breath came fast and heavy. I totally wanted this. I'd wanted to experience his touch for nearly ten years. 'Yes.'

'Yes, what?' He ground his cock against my middle. 'Say it, Ivy.'

'I want this, Liam. I always have.'

He stroked a finger along the outside of my damp panties, circling my clit. 'Me too, baby. I want all of you.' He leaned in, his hot breath against my ear. 'I want you to be mine. Forever.'

I nodded. In that moment, I would've signed over my heart to Liam Cole if it weren't already his.

I arched my back as he hooked a finger either side of my panties and slid them down with my pants, tossing the clothes aside. He unhooked my bra and dropped it to the floor. I stood completely naked in front of him for the first time, and the intense hunger in Liam's gaze made my heart flutter like crazy.

His finger slid between my legs, spreading the moisture. 'Fuck, Ivy,' he groaned. 'You're so wet.'

He stroked up and down my clit. My knees buckled and Liam wrapped an arm around my waist, supporting me. He nibbled on the fleshy tip of my ear while circling his finger over my swollen bud.

I climbed higher and higher as the tension built.

Just when I thought I would internally combust, Liam lowered to his knees. I inhaled a sharp breath.

'Liam … I …' My entire body pulsed with need. 'I can't take … anymore.'

He looked up at me, raw possession burning in his eyes. 'Yes you can, baby. I've wanted to taste you for so long.'

Holding my gaze, Liam hooked my leg over his shoulder before sliding a finger inside my pussy. I moaned, forcing my palms flat against the wall to steady myself. He glided the finger out and slipped two back in.

'Oh, God!' I groaned, rocking against his hand to increase the friction.

'That's it, Ivy. Come for me.'

Before I had a chance to reply, Liam's tongue swept over my clit. He licked and sucked while sliding his fingers in and out, curling them deep inside me. I fisted his hair, holding him in place, desperate for release. The coil of tension grew and grew. Tighter and tighter until roaring heat flashed through my body. Billions of tiny stars exploded behind my lids as I crashed over the edge, screaming his name.

Withdrawing and lowering my leg, Liam stood, effortlessly lifting me and locking my legs around his waist. I rolled my hips, rubbing my clit against his hardness.

A low and wild growl rumbled in his chest. Taking my mouth in a hungry kiss, he carried me to the couch and sat down with me straddling his hips. The taste of him mixed with a hint of me sent more moisture trickling between my legs.

Liam cupped my jaw between his hands. 'I've fantasised about making love to you, so many fucking times.' His thumb brushed along my lower lip. 'How it would feel sliding inside your heat. How you would taste.'

I tilted forward, gliding my wetness along the outside of his cock. I couldn't wait any longer. 'I need you, Liam.'

He gripped my hips, holding me in place. 'Baby, if you keep doing that, I'm gonna come before we get the chance.'

That damn dimple returned and my soul burst into flames.

Snatching his wallet from inside his jacket, Liam ripped out a condom and slid it on. He lifted my hips slightly, hovering the head of his cock at my entrance. My gaze locked with his and in that moment, the world around us skidded to a halt. Only Liam and I existed.

I lowered, sliding down his length, stretching and widening to accommodate his size.

Liam growled, tightening his hold on my hips. 'Ivy … *fuck.*'

I lifted again, then slipped back down, finding a slow and steady rhythm. With each glide, my breasts rubbed against the light sheen of sweat on his chest, heightening the sensations.

He nipped at the side of my neck. 'You feel like heaven. I want this every day for the rest of our lives.'

I froze.

Shit. What the hell was I doing? So caught up in the pleasure, I forgot what was happening.

Liam pinched my chin. 'Baby, what's wrong?'

'It's just …' I tried to look away, but he held my head in place.

'Tell me, Ivy.'

The words needed to be said, I needed to get them out. Liam deserved to know how I felt.

'I'm scared.' My eyes filled with tears.

He brushed a strand of hair from my face. 'Don't be scared, baby. Every time I think of my future, I see you in it. I love you, Ivy.'

'Forever's a long time, Liam. What if in forty years from now, you don't want the old and grey version of me?'

'There will never be a time when I won't want you.' He planted a gentle kiss on my lips and it bled into my soul.

'Once I claim you, we'll live a long and happy life together, ageing at the same rate.' He paused. 'Ivy, you're the only one for me.'

He'd told me this before, but only now was I ready to hear it.

Warmth spread through my chest. Hope that we could have a future, despite our different worlds, despite the challenges we might face.

Was I finally ready to say yes?

Liam wiped away a fallen tear with his thumb.

I couldn't keep avoiding him, hiding my feelings behind a mask, pretending the longing I felt had nothing to do with him. I couldn't keep living half a life, because the thought of losing Liam forever crippled me.

It was time I stopped running.

Leaning down, I kissed him, pouring my heart and soul into his. My hips rocked, gliding up and down his cock. It felt so good, like we were meant to be together, as though every moment we'd ever shared had led us to this point. I moved faster. Grinding harder until only the sounds of our moans and our bodies sliding together filled the hut.

Liam slowed, taking my palm and holding it flat against his thumping heart. 'I'll always be yours, Ivy.' His gaze locked with mine. 'Say you'll be mine.'

Liam was all I'd ever wanted. My heart had known it since I was ten years old, but only now was I ready to tear off that mask for good.

'Yes, I love you,' I breathed, my heart clenching. 'I'm yours, Liam. Forever.'

Explosions of pleasure ripped through my body and I screamed out his name, clenching his cock inside me.

'Ivy,' he growled, thrusting harder as he came with me. '*Mine.*'

Unmasked

____

KRISTIN SILK

ANNA SLID behind her desk to find a coffee waiting for her as there had been every work day since Clarke started as her personal assistant a year ago. She'd told him a million times she didn't expect it, but that hadn't deterred him. Even before she took the first sip, she knew it would be just the way she liked it. A small sigh of satisfaction escaped her as the caffeine hit. How did he always know exactly what she needed?

He appeared at the door then, leaning casually against it, pushing his glasses up his nose and his dark hair out of his eyes. 'How's your coffee?'

They played this game every morning. 'Perfect. As you well know.'

He grinned, and her stomach did a flippy little twist like it always did.

'Anything else you need?' His dark eyes regarded her softly.

There were so many things that came to mind at that question, none of which were appropriate to ask of your PA.

'No thanks, Clarke. Just shut the door, please.'

As the door clicked shut, she dropped her forehead to her hands, her newly dyed crimson strands falling between her fingers. God, he was gorgeous. If she weren't his boss and a decade older than him … but she was. And nothing would change those cold, hard facts.

Attempting to calm the fluttering in her stomach, she opened her laptop and started checking emails.

LILLIAN ENTERED Anna's office with a file under one arm, casting a glance at the silver mask hanging from the bunch of twisted twigs that passed for a floral arrangement. 'Going to the masquerade ball, then?'

Clarke had convinced her to buy it last week when a stallholder had been selling them on the street near their office building. It had instantly appealed to her, the smooth silver top with semi circles like fish scales on the bottom half. It reminded her of her own inner mask—slippery as quicksilver but strong as steel.

'Oh, I don't know. What about you?'

'Myra and I have a special anniversary that day. Thirty years together. So, we're having dinner at a fancy restaurant.'

'Thirty years. That's special.'

Her boss's eyes softened in a way they rarely did at work.

'It is.' She pointed the file at Anna. 'But you should go. I went last year and it was a hoot.'

'I've got a lot of work to do.'

Lillian raised her eyebrows. 'No work is that important. You work too hard. Go, have some fun.'

There was a knock on her partly opened door and Clarke stuck his head in, reminding her of her ten o'clock appointment. The smile he gave her made her heart gallop against her rib cage.

Lillian watched him head back to his desk outside the office. She handed the file to Anna. 'That boy is so hot for you. You really should do something about that.'

Carefully smoothing her features into studied indifference, Anna's heart sank.

You really should do something about that. She didn't need to ask what that meant. It meant, don't encourage him, or maybe, actively dissuade him. She knew her boss was right. It wasn't fair to lead him on when there was no possible future in it for either of them.

Lillian's phone went off. She pointed to the file as she left. 'I need it by five o'clock today.' The door clicked closed behind her.

Maybe it had been Lillian's way of reminding her what a bad idea it would be to go out with a younger work colleague. She'd been the one who'd found Anna falling apart in her office after Brett started going out with Tanya from accounts, five minutes after unceremoniously dumping her. Anna's professional facade had fooled everyone else. They all thought she'd moved on. Lillian was the only one who knew the truth.

She had moved on eventually, but it had been a painful lesson and not one she would forget in a hurry. But, as she stared at the closed door, all she could think about was Clarke's smile and the way he sent shivers through her every time he looked at her.

***

The next day, Lillian left a job advertisement for Anna to pass on to Clarke. As if she was giving her a shove to "do something about that". Anna stared at the sheet of paper. What if he went for it? What if he got it? Her stomach twisted at the thought.

Get a hold of yourself.

She took a deep breath. Time to bring out the big guns and remind herself again why a younger man was a bad idea. She needed to look no further than her own father for that—eleven years younger than her mum, he'd left them both for a younger woman when Anna had been fourteen, leaving her to be the responsible adult when her mum fell apart. He'd moved on, starting a family with his new woman, and after a few sporadic attempts to keep in touch, virtually forgot about Anna and her mother.

Rubbing her temples with her fingertips, she gritted her teeth.

And then there was Brett. How much proof did she need that younger men were bound to move on to the next shiny, or younger, thing? She hadn't been enough for either of them and despite what her hormones were telling her, she wouldn't be enough for Clarke either. He was twenty-two for crying out loud.

She exhaled heavily. *Just take the damn paper out to him.*

Finding him at his desk, she allowed herself a moment to watch before interrupting. His slender fingers tapped the keyboard, the backs of his large hands, lightly freckled. His crisp, white shirt sleeves were rolled up to his elbows, exposing muscular forearms. The top couple of buttons were undone, revealing a hint of dark chest hair. Her traitorous fingers twitched with the urge to touch him, to stroke that dark hair and follow it all the way down.

Damn it. Focus. 'Can I talk to you for a minute?'

Clarke flashed her a brilliant smile. 'I'm all yours.'

Gah! Her insides slid around like an uncooked egg. She swallowed. 'There's a position coming up that you might want to apply for.'

His smile faded.

She resisted the urge to smooth the wrinkle between his eyebrows. It was for his own good after all.

'It's as an assistant to David Grophy.'

Clarke made a sound of disgust. 'I don't want to work for old Gropey.'

She forced out her best boss voice. 'You really shouldn't keep calling him that. One day he's going to hear you.'

'I'll stop calling him that when he stops being such a creep.'

Well, she couldn't argue with that. The man had the nickname for good reason. But she pressed on. 'Given he's the big boss, it would mean you'd have more opportunities.'

Clarke stared at his computer screen and started typing.

'Clarke.'

He glanced at her, his jaw tight.

'It would also mean a pay rise for you.'

He stared at his screen again as if she weren't there.

'Clarke.'

'Are you unhappy with my work?' he said, still not looking at her.

'Of course not. You're the best PA I've ever had. I don't know what I'd do without you.' Professionally speaking, of course.

He turned to her and the hurt in his eyes hit her like a punch. 'Have I done something,to upset you?'

'Of course not. No.'

His eyes flicked to the top button of her shirt. 'Then why are you trying to get rid of me?'

'I'm not. I just don't want to hold you back from what might be a great opportunity for you.'

'Well, then, I'm not interested.'

'You should at least read it.' She pointed to the paper

beside him, but maddeningly, he'd gone back to staring at his computer.

Shaking her head, Anna walked towards her office but turned in time to see him scrunching up the paper and hurling it into the bin beneath his desk.

She'd failed robustly to adhere to Lillian's request. But she couldn't help the way her heart did crazy backflips of joy that he didn't want to leave her.

***

Anna's next opportunity to "do something about that" came at the end of the following day.

Standing at the entrance of her office, Clarke pushed his glasses up his nose and cleared his throat. 'So, a few of the others are going out for Chinese and to check out a new club afterwards. Do you want to come?'

By "a few others" she knew he meant a group his own age.

Her heart twisted. Lillian's words had been on repeat in her head all day. Maybe this was the perfect opportunity to define the boundaries of their relationship.

'I'm sure they wouldn't want someone my age hanging around. Plus, I'm also their boss.'

He frowned. 'Anna, you're thirty-two, not one hundred and thirty-two. And it's outside of work, so who cares if you're the boss.'

She swallowed. 'I don't want to kill the party.'

He took a step towards her. 'You wouldn't.' After a pause, he said, 'What if it was just the two of us? What if I ditched them and we went somewhere for dinner?'

This was the moment. She had to do what was best for him despite her own feelings. Her heart clawed its way up her throat, trying to burst out, but she swallowed the 'yes' down with a gulp. 'I … I can't Clarke.'

He stared at her, his eyes a mixture of confusion and

sadness. She wanted to reach for him, to bury her face in his chest, to inhale the musky scent of him. Instead, she put all her attention into holding her professional mask in place, even though cracks were already appearing.

He sighed heavily and turned away, lifting his satchel onto one shoulder. 'Bye, then.'

'Bye.' Her voice was barely audible.

He turned and stalked down the corridor, her heart bouncing along after him as if attached by a string.

As his long-legged stride took him further and further away from her, Anna swallowed the urge to cry. She'd done the right thing, hadn't she? The only possible thing. So why did it feel like someone had stuck a knife in her heart and twisted?

***

The irony of arriving at work sleep deprived wasn't lost on her. She may as well have been out partying instead of lying awake all night, torturing herself, imagining Clarke's hands and lips on another woman.

And worse, he turned up on time when he was usually early.

It was ridiculous that she felt like crying because he hadn't made her coffee. The teaspoon clinked despondently against her ceramic cup.

'Sorry I didn't make your coffee.'

At his voice, flashes of energy sparked down her spine. Stupid sparks.

'I've told you before there's no need to do that. I'm perfectly capable of making my own.' Her voice came out robotic, tight and expressionless. She channelled Business Anna and tried to sound normal.

'So, have a good night?' Her voice was overly cheery now, as if she were compensating for the previous flatness.

God, what was wrong with her? It was as if he hadn't asked her out.

'Are you okay?' Clarke leaned against the bench, his long legs crossed at the ankles, looking annoyingly, utterly delectable.

Damn him and his freaky X-ray vision, seeing through the facade that fooled everyone else. 'I'm fine. Why wouldn't I be?'

'I don't know. You just seem a little …'

Striding back into her office, she pressed the heels of her hands against her forehead. No mask was big enough to contain all this shit.

LATER THAT MORNING, hearing Darren at Clarke's desk, Anna eavesdropped shamelessly from behind her partly open door.

'Last night was a cracker, hey.'

Clarke's answering murmur was indecipherable.

'Dude, Bianca was all over you. She's totally hot for you. You should be tapping that.'

Anna froze, the sheaf of papers she held falling to the floor with a soft whooshing sound that drowned out Clarke's reply.

Her heart seized in her chest. She pressed a hand over the ache.

Then she heard Darren's voice again. 'Oh, that's right. You've got a thing for your boss.'

Clarke's reply was clear enough this time. 'Shut up, Darren.'

'You've got a thing for grannies, haven't you? What's up, Clarko? She can't be that hard to catch. Surely she can't run that fast.'

'I said shut the fuck up, dickhead!'

Anna ran out to see the two men shoving each other in the corridor. Darren punched Clarke who fell to the floor.

'Stop!' Seeing Clarke on the floor, clutching his side, his glasses beside him, had her control melting faster than an ice cream cake on a bonfire. 'Darren, what the hell are you doing?'

He held both arms out to the sides. 'He attacked me for no reason.'

Lillian's voice shot through the corridor like a bullet. 'I sincerely doubt that, Mr Aims.' She'd used her quiet voice, the one that contained a world of cold fury.

Darren gaped, all bluster and fake innocence.

Lillian gave him a ball-shrivelling look. 'My office. Now.'

He hunched his shoulders and followed her.

'Anna, you take care of Clarke,' Lillian shot over her shoulder.

She helped Clarke into her office. 'You damned idiot! You could have been hurt.'

'He said …'

'I heard what he said.'

'You did?' Clarke ran a hand through his hair. 'Don't listen to him, Anna. He's a dickhead. Age means nothing. It's just a number.'

'Oh, I don't know. A couple of twenty-two-year-old men fighting in the corridor sounds pretty age appropriate to me.'

His soft brown eyes pleaded with her. 'I'm not like that, okay. Don't put me in the same box as him.'

A silence stretched between them. Clarke bit his lip, watching her cautiously.

She tried to resist asking—God knows she did—but, as she was fast learning, resistance was futile when it came to Clarke.

She stared at his collar. 'So, you and Bianca, huh?'

The light tone she'd aimed for, flopped totally. Her words came out sounding pathetically jealous.

Something inscrutable flickered in his eyes. 'Since when do you care?'

Her cheeks burned. 'Of course. It's none of my business.'

He held her arm when she would have turned away and looked deep into her eyes. 'Nothing happened. She wanted it to, but I didn't. We're just friends.'

His hand slid down her arm, igniting every cell with his touch.

'I wish I'd come with you last night.' The words were out before she could stop them.

His eyes softened. 'Me too. I missed you.'

Her heart almost burst out of her chest at his words. Did this mean they had a chance? That she hadn't ruined everything after all?

He moved closer, wincing a little.

'Are you hurt?'

'He got me in the ribs. I'm fine.'

'Do you want me to take a look at it?' What the hell was she doing? She had no first aid qualifications whatsoever and they both knew it.

The heat between them shimmered.

He cleared his throat. 'Actually, now you mention it, it is quite sore. Maybe you could look at it.'

Holding her gaze, he untucked his shirt.

Her pulse raced. God, was she insane? She slid her hands along the bottom of his shirt, trying to lift it. 'I might need to undo your buttons.'

'Yeah. You should do that.' His voice was husky.

She started on his top button. The combination of nervousness and lust made undoing it almost impossible.

'I'll help. There's a lot of buttons.' He started from the bottom and they met in the middle.

She unpeeled his shirt to reveal his lean, muscular chest, covered with a smattering of dark hair. He smelled so good, clean and musky that she wanted to inhale him.

Still keeping up the ridiculous charade, she looked carefully at the area he indicated, trailing her fingers gently over it. 'Can't see anything.'

When she straightened, he stared at her lips. 'Are you going to kiss it better?'

'Do you want me to?'

'Do you even have to ask?' The hunger in his eyes gave her the confidence to do exactly what she wanted. She pressed her lips to the side of his chest, savouring the warmth of his skin.

His sharp intake of breath was satisfying.

'Sore?'

'That's definitely helping.'

She kissed him again. 'Here?'

'Mmm.'

'What about here?'

'Uh-huh.'

After she kissed him a few more times, she finally gave in to the urge and licked him.

He groaned deeply. 'Fuck.'

She straightened and stared at him. His whole body radiated tension. He tossed his glasses on her desk.

'You missed somewhere.' His voice was raspy and so sexy she wanted to rub her entire body against him.

She raised an eyebrow in question and he pointed to his mouth. Lifting her lips to his, she kissed him softly. It should have felt awkward, kissing someone new after all this time. But it didn't. It felt like coming home.

His lips moved gently over hers, soft drugging kisses.

She moaned into his mouth and his arms tightened around her, pulling her closer, winding his fingers into her hair. The scent of him, the taste almost drove her insane. She wanted to eat him alive. Winding her arms around his waist, she stroked up and down his bare back, his muscles bunching under her hands.

They clutched at each other, the kiss deepening until their tongues were sliding together, hot and wet. Her nipples threatened to break the confines of her clothing, pressing out in tight, needy peaks. The deep throbbing ache between her legs had her pressing against his obvious arousal.

Finally, they broke for air and stood, breathing hard, staring at each other, his eyes unfocused and heavy-lidded.

Her office door opened, and Lillian walked in backwards, talking to someone outside.

Anna stumbled back a step. 'Clarke, you're …'

An impressive bulge strained at the front of his pants.

Grabbing his glasses from the desk, she held them while he adjusted himself. He'd just slid them on when Lillian turned to face them.

She frowned. 'Clarke, why is your shirt undone?'

His mouth opened and closed. 'Uh …'

'Oh, I was just …' *What, genius? Giving him mouth to mouth?* Anna cleared her throat. 'I was just checking … to see if he was injured.'

Lillian took a step towards Clarke as he did up his buttons. 'Are you okay? I'm the first-aid officer. I can have a look at it if you need.'

'No, it's fine. It was sore at first, but Anna had a look at it and it feels much better now.'

'Well, I hope she read you the riot act. You know I won't tolerate fighting or any other kind of imbecilic behaviour at work.'

He nodded, keeping a completely straight face. 'Yeah, she really gave it to me.'

'Good.'

It was only when Lillian's back was turned that Anna saw the twitch at the corners of his mouth and the twinkle in his eyes.

***

Later that day, Lillian regarded her with narrowed eyes. 'Did you do anything about Clarke?'

'Uh …' Anna shuffled papers on her desk. How could she tell her boss the truth? That despite everything, she'd fallen hard and was done holding back her feelings for him.

Lillian's voice softened. 'Honey, I've seen how you look at each other. How hard can it be? Just ask him out.'

Anna stared at her boss, a mixture of confusion and horror swirling inside her. 'You didn't mean put him off?'

'Of course not. I meant go on a date or something. Explore what's between you.'

Ah, hell. Thank God she'd failed in her attempts to cool things off between them. Her neck and cheeks burned. 'Well, in that case, I'm working on it.'

Lillian's face split in a wide grin. 'Atta girl.'

***

The masquerade ball was in full swing when she arrived, the conference room transformed into a wonderland, the dimness punctuated by twinkling fairy lights and candles on every table.

But everything faded at the sight of the tall, dark-haired man striding towards her. A slick, black mask hid the top of his face, but there was no mistaking that crooked smile.

Her pulse leapt to heart attack level. 'You don't have your glasses on.'

'Contacts.' He took her hand. 'I was worried you weren't going to show.'

He stroked his thumb over the back of her hand and her nerves fluttered into overdrive.

After a drink, they danced.

He held her close and her nervousness melted away. They kept their own slow-swaying rhythm that had nothing to do with the music. One hand held hers while the other caressed the small of her back, fingers splayed as if he wanted to feel as much of her as possible.

His breath tickled her ear. 'I really want to kiss you.'

She tilted her chin in invitation and he pressed his lips against hers. She kissed him back, slow and deep, melting against him like butter on hot toast.

She wanted him now and forever and didn't want to wait to let him know. 'Want to go somewhere more private?'

A slow, sexy smile was his reply. He kept his hand on the small of her back as they made a hasty exit.

The fluorescent lights of the corridor made her blink. He stroked her fingers. 'We could go to my place.'

'I don't think I can wait that long.'

When she spotted the door to a utility room, she pulled him in, locked the door and flicked on the light. There were vacuum cleaners and cleaning appliances and it smelled like disinfectant. But she didn't care. She needed him like oxygen.

Clarke cupped her face. 'I want you so bad.'

'I want you too.'

They kissed then, long and slow and deep. She slid her hands over his chest, pulling his shirt out of his pants.

Her mask felt suddenly tight and restrictive. As if reading her mind, he pulled his own mask off and then hers.

'I need to see you.'

He kissed her again with a slow, burning urgency.

She unbuttoned his shirt and pressed her face into his chest, inhaling the scent of him. She kissed him, running her hands over the coarse hair.

He cupped her breast and she sighed. Then he slid his hands up her thighs and under the flared skirt of her dress, tracing the outline of her underwear with his fingers.

Turning her, he kissed the side of her neck. As he unzipped her dress he chased the cold metal with hot kisses down the length of her spine. The silky material caressed her skin as it slid down her body, and he placed her dress carefully on an industrial-looking vacuum cleaner.

She unzipped his pants, sliding them with his underwear down his thighs, his impressive erection springing free. She cupped his balls, kneading gently, tracing the hard length of him until he groaned.

He removed her bra and pushed her underwear down her legs, the slow deliberate slide setting her whole body on fire. Her high heels made her feel sexy, so she left them on.

The hunger and reverence in Clarke's eyes undid her.

'Fuck, Anna, you're gorgeous.'

He crushed her to him, giving her a scorching open-mouthed kiss that had them both breathing hard.

'Tell me what you want.' Clarke nibbled her earlobe, making it almost impossible to form words.

'You. Inside me. Now.'

The room was tiny, with limited space. She turned her back to him and braced her hands against the wall. 'Like this.'

His hands roamed everywhere, stroking her breasts, her stomach, sliding between her legs into her slick wetness. She moaned, the heaviness of his erection sliding against where she ached for him.

'Condom.' The word came out a pant.

He reached for his pants and she heard the crinkle of the foil packet as he sheathed himself, protecting them both.

She widened her stance to give him access, the anticipation of feeling him inside her almost more than she could bear.

He kissed her neck. The blunt nudge of him against her entrance made her hold her breath as she waited for him to slide in.

She felt a deliciously gentle stretch as he slid the tip of himself in. Then he slid back out. And did it again.

'What are you doing?' She tried to push back to bring him into her.

He held her hips. 'Does that feel good?'

When he did it again—a slow, gentle pulse followed by the drag of pleasure as he slid all the way out—a breathless 'yes' was all she could manage.

'Then just relax. Let me love you, Anna.'

Again. A lingering, shallow slide in and out. And she realised. He was extending her pleasure. He was *loving* her.

The concentration of that tiny movement focused all her attention there. Each deliberate caress magnified the need in all the places he hadn't yet reached. Again and again.

He loved her so slowly, so tenderly, that something inside her snapped and unravelled, and the fist around her heart loosened and fell away. A sob escaped her.

He stilled. 'Okay, babe?'

She nodded. She'd never been more okay in her life. 'Oh, Clarke.'

'I've got you.' He kissed her shoulder, sliding in a little further now, the ripples of the tiny movement echoing through her entire body. The smooth glide set off sparks like a firecracker inside her, taking her right to the edge until she trembled. She moaned deeply.

His breath laboured in her ear. Finally, he slid all the way in and they both moaned in pleasure. He held her tight against him, now still.

'Clarke?'

His voice was tight. 'Don't move, babe. I just need a moment. Otherwise I'm not going to last.'

They stood for a moment, pressed together with him deep inside her, his chest against her back. She turned her head and kissed him—this beautiful, sexy man. Why had she ever resisted him? His hands stroked her breasts, squeezing her nipples gently, creating a zap of sensation in her core. He slid one hand down to where they were joined, stroking her just where she needed it.

But it wasn't enough.

'Clarke. Move.'

After a couple of smooth slow strokes, he gave her exactly what she wanted, thrusting deeper and faster, hitting the sweet spot inside her until she was mindless with desire. She didn't recognise the noises that came out of her —and didn't care. She braced herself as her orgasm built, lifting her higher and higher until she burst. A thousand stars exploded inside her as she clenched around him, plea-sure rippling through her in waves, her cries of ecstasy echoing off the walls of the tiny room.

Clarke was right behind her as he thrust deep and shuddered against her with a low groan. 'Holy fuck!'

Her arms and legs sagged like overcooked noodles, and only Clarke's firm arm around her waist stopped her from toppling headfirst into a mop bucket.

He held her tight against him as they breathed heavily. When he withdrew, leaving her body to toss the condom in a nearby bin, she made a small noise of protest. He was back straight away, turning her to him, kissing her gently, holding her tight.

'I don't think my legs work.' She wobbled in her heels.

He found a disused milk crate and turned it over, tossing his pants over it and sitting down. He reached for her and she sank onto his lap. His arms stroked gently up and down her back as he kissed her neck, her ear, her lips, tenderly.

She pulled away and looked into his eyes, every last shred of resistance gone.

He looked dazed. 'That was …' He shook his head in wonder. 'Woah.'

'Yeah.' She smiled at him. 'It was.'

She stroked his jaw. She hoped he could see it in her eyes, but she wanted to give him the words, too. 'I love you.'

His eyes softened and went suspiciously shiny. 'I love you too, Anna, so much.' He pressed his face into her neck. Then pulled back, wiping his cheeks. 'Ah, crap.'

'Are you okay?'

'It's just … hearing you say it after all this time.' He put a hand over his heart.

'Oh.' Her own eyes got misty. 'I wish I'd said it sooner.'

He cupped her face. 'I didn't want you to say it unless you meant it. But I've got to admit, I'm relieved. I was starting to think I'd grossly overestimated my charm.'

She chuckled softly. 'No, you didn't. You grossly underestimated my powers of resistance.'

'It only took me a year to win you over.' His crooked smile melted her. 'Oops. We trashed our masks.' He held up his, which had a rip from the bottom to the corner of one eye.

'Oh no. It must have been my heels.'

He tossed it into the bin. 'Doesn't matter. It did its job.

Got me the girl.' He gave her a cheeky grin. 'Yours is probably okay if you want to keep it. It's a bit scuffed but not too wrecked.' He handed it to her.

She traced the silver outline for a moment, a representation of the mask she'd worn to keep herself safe for so long.

'Nah.' She tossed it into the bin on top of Clarke's. 'I don't need it anymore.'

They held each other, stroking each other's skin softly. When she looked deep into Clarke's soft, soulful eyes, she knew she would never need a mask again.

No Rules

____

DAVINA STONE

'YOUR ROOM IS on the top floor. The bathroom's shared with my sis. She can hog it for hours, but if you need a slash, tell her to get lost.'

Ethan tossed his friend Luke a grin. 'Yeah right, as if I'd turf her out in her own home.'

Luke rolled his eyes. 'Nah, don't worry. She's a freakin' prima donna, but she won't bite. Grab your stuff, I'll take you up.'

Ethan eyeballed the majestic sweep of the staircase. His jaw had already hit the ground a few minutes earlier when the chauffeured car headed along the driveway of his best mate's home. Even in the dark, the grounds looked bigger than the outback town he came from.

At boarding school—the most elite boys' school in Perth—they all wore uniforms, so it wasn't that obvious that Ethan was the kid from the bush on a scholarship. Being brilliant at rugby did the rest.

And now he'd jagged a weekend at his best mate's holiday house in Margaret River. Yeah, finally made it into the inner sanctum of the super cool dudes.

Three flights of stairs later, Luke flung open a door and flicked on the lights.

Ethan gave a low whistle. 'All mine?'

Luke chuckled. 'Well, you could ask Naomi to join you.'

'Naomi?'

'My sis.'

'Oh.'

Luke smirked. 'Joke. She's nineteen and only dates guys with Porsches.'

'Right.' Ethan swallowed hard. 'Rules me out then.'

The thought of bumping into Naomi in the bathroom scared the crap out of him, which was kind of funny given the circumstances.

'Early start tomorrow. Surf'll be pumping.' Luke pointed to a door opposite and waggled his eyebrows. 'Bathroom. You've been warned.'

'Cool.' Ethan gave a thumbs up.

Left alone, he took a quick turn of the sumptuously furnished room then unpacked. He'd forgotten to bring anything to wear in bed. Too bad, he'd be fine in a pair of boxers, it was only two nights after all. Grabbing his toothbrush, toothpaste and the guest towel off the bed, he tiptoed across to the bathroom. An arc of light shone through a crack in the door.

He ground to a halt, heart hammering.

Was Naomi in there? Ethan crept forward, barely breathing, curious as to what this bathroom princess looked like.

A long, soft moan froze him to the spot.

Shit on wheels! Was Naomi fucking some Porsche guy in there?

His breathing ragged, Ethan ordered his legs to back off, so why in fuck's name was he edging closer? He plastered one eye to the slither of light, giving him a wider view of the room.

Oh Jesus freakin' Christ! The breath hissed from his lips.

Alone. Naked. Long legs splayed wide, her butt hitched onto the edge of the bath, one foot braced on the closed seat of the toilet and a mane of golden hair tumbling around her shoulders, this had to be *her*. And …

Oh fuck! One hand curled tight around the edge of the bath while the other worked her … her … unbelievably beautiful pussy.

Ethan's cock rocketed, pushing hard at the minimal restraint of his boxers, eyes rivetted to those dipping, swirling fingers.

Involuntarily, he freed himself and matched his strokes to hers, holding his breath, terrified of making a sound as a volcano threatened in his groin.

Biting back harsh puffs, he stared unblinking as Naomi's thighs trembled and fell wider, hips gyrating, breasts jiggling, nipples like ripe cherries on peachy mounds of flesh. Whimpers escaped her, a pulse throbbed in her neck, glistening fingers moving so fast they were almost a blur. Nathan's hand stroked frenziedly over his swollen slippery tip as his pulse went crazy and his balls felt like they were about to shoot out of his engorged cock.

With a guttural cry, Naomi shattered, legs scissoring around her fingers as her whole body convulsed with her orgasm.

That did it.

Ethan bit back the desperate need to shout out all kinds of inappropriate words as he came like a freight train, trying to contain it in his hand and failing miserably as a sea of semen arced onto his stomach and chest.

Holy. Fucking. *Shit!*

Fighting the urge to stay as Naomi slid limply onto the

floor and panicking that she'd catch him, Ethan did a speed-shuffle back to his room and shut the door as quietly as a guy could when he was covered up to his eyeballs in his own come.

Only when he leaned safely against the door, panting and rubbing himself dry with his towel, was he able to focus.

How in crap's name could he face Naomi at breakfast, or wherever else he might see her over the weekend, knowing he'd simultaneously come with her? What if she'd spotted him? No, she couldn't have. He'd die, he'd freakin' die if she found out.

He'd been brought up to respect girls, so what did this make him?

He couldn't tell anyone, not a whisper.

Ever.

And worse—how could any girl on the planet be that beautiful? 'Cos now, he'd compare every other woman to her for the rest of his life, and none would ever measure up.

And finally, Ethan racked his brain, how the fuck was he going to get a truckload of semen out of his guest towel?

TEN YEARS LATER

Naomi Lawrence smiled at the sound of her stiletto heels as she crossed the marbled foyer. God, she loved the sharp *tap-tap* of her fast-moving feet, the way her calves tightened with each step, and the way her suit was so perfectly tailored to her body it sheathed her like a second skin.

This, Naomi told herself, was power.

Sweet revenge.

Hadn't the late, *great* Jasper Lawrence always ridiculed her? Called her a bimbo airhead who would never make anything of herself? And now she had her own empire, based wholly on her range of lip products.

NAO-ME, a play on her name that she'd turned into an international brand.

'Sit on that, Dad, and rotate,' she whispered under her breath as she pressed the elevator button to take her to the top floor, the domain of NAO-ME Bold and Beautiful Lips.

Tap, tap, tap, past the reception desk with the scroll of pouty lips blowing kisses on a wide screen behind, heels rendered soundless as she stepped onto the plush carpet of her office suite.

Skirting her desk and sinking into leather, Naomi flicked on the computer as her personal assistant Lou sashayed in with her standard almond milk macchiato.

Oddly, for first thing on a Monday when Naomi usually demanded an hour of quiet time, Lou wasn't reading the signs.

Naomi glanced up with a raised eyebrow. 'Hmm?'

'You still haven't given me a name.' It was more a demand than a request.

Naomi scooted her chair closer to the desk. 'Really, Lou? Must we do this now?'

Lou, who'd worked for her since the inception of NAO-ME, stood her ground. 'Yep. We must.'

Naomi sighed heavily. 'I'll go on my own.'

'No way!' Lou's green eyes skewered her. 'What happens to NAO-ME's credibility if the Queen of Lips doesn't have a partner at her own charity ball?'

'For fuck's sake, Lou, you're a Rottweiler.'

'Yep, you pay me to be.'

Naomi narrowed her gaze and faked interest in the computer screen.

'What about Ethan Cowan?' Lou's tone was casual, *way* too casual.

Naomi stiffened. Ethan Cowan. Her brother's friend and now the darling of the professional rugby world. The one guy who'd fuelled her X-rated fantasies and single-handedly ran the batteries down on her vibrator for years.

Tell-tale heat fanned up her neck. 'No way!'

'Oh, come on. He's mega-gorgeous, mega-famous and you know him through Luke. Think of the publicity.'

Naomi could sense Lou smirking. She focused on the three hundred new email notifications and tried to breathe normally.

'I'll take that as a yes.' Lou headed for the door. 'I'll contact him on your behalf,' she tossed over her shoulder.

Naomi grabbed her macchiato and choked on a mouthful.

'TO THANK you all for coming, it's my pleasure to present to you the amazing Naomi Lawrence, founder of NAO-ME.'

The compere's voice boomed through the venue as Naomi skipped up to the podium.

She wasn't sure what she said or how long she talked for, she was just thankful to be away from her table, giving her body a rest from its crazy reaction to Ethan Cowan sitting next to her.

Even now, in front of this crowd of beautiful people, faces half obscured by elaborate masks, she was painfully aware of him in her periphery, broad shoulders almost bursting out of his tux as he lounged back in his chair. The clean, hard angle of his jaw and cheekbones, and the sensual curve of his upper lip divinely accentuated by a simple black mask.

All night he'd been so attentive, so charming. And he smelt intoxicating, subtle expensive cologne mingling with his own musky male scent. When he leaned in to catch what she'd said over the hubbub of three hundred revellers, his arm had bumped hers deliciously. That bicep felt like it was made of some kind of precious metal, and a perfectly fitted white dress shirt slid over pecs she guessed would be diamond hard.

She was wet for him, wasn't she? Desire pulsed between her thighs at those insignificant little frissons of contact.

Except it could only ever work in her fantasies. However much she craved Ethan in her bed, she would sleep alone tonight.

All this went through Naomi's head, even as she trotted out her spiel of how NAO-ME had become one of the most successful cosmetic brands worldwide, and how The NAO-ME Ball was raising money for women's refuges around Australia.

As she took her seat to rousing applause, Ethan leaned in close, his breath stirring tendrils of hair from the elaborate updo that had taken three hours for the hairdresser to style this afternoon.

'You were amazing.' His husky tone sent shudders of delight arrowing into her sex.

She found herself giggling. 'Oh, thank you.'

Behaving like an infatuated schoolgirl, Naomi. Shut the hell up.

'Not afraid of public speaking, then?' His mouth tugged sideways, made her want to place her lips right there, where that sexy twist met equally sexy stubble.

She widened her eyes behind her mask. 'Should I be?'

Ethan shrugged. 'You'd be amazed how many people say they'd prefer to die than speak in public.'

She laughed lightly. 'Not one of my phobias.'

Storm grey eyes held hers. 'So, what is?'

Naomi swallowed hard. His eyes remained unblinking behind the mask. Could he see into her soul? Her gaze fixed on his lips and she imagined them all over her. She stifled a moan, bit back the urge to let her tongue moisten her lips in invitation.

'Maybe I don't have one. Maybe I'm perfect,' she clipped out, trying to be flippant only to feel like a swollen-headed arse.

Elbows on the table now, he watched her intensely. 'I think maybe you are.'

Her blood pulsed and she thanked her guardian angel when the band started up a second later.

'And *maybe*, you'd like to dance with me?' Ethan raised his voice over the volume.

Naomi's heart hammered along with the thump of the bass notes. Thankfully, it wasn't a slow number. '*Maybe* I would, Mr Cowan.'

He stood, she stood. For a bare moment, their bodies fused—the heat of Ethan's thigh burning into hers, the softness of her breast meeting the wall of his torso. She heard him inhale sharply.

Her breathing went haywire, before Ethan stepped back.

'After you,' he said, lips curling into a smile that hit the sweet spot with deadly precision.

ON THE DANCE floor among the bobbing, laughing crowd, Naomi feasted on Ethan from behind the safety of her mask. God, the guy could move! Guess he wasn't captain of the Western Valour rugby team for nothing. And judging by the way other women *accidentally* came close, lips pouting, eyes hungry behind their disguises, she wasn't the only one to notice.

He was a magnet.

No doubt, Ethan could fuck any woman he wanted here tonight.

But it wouldn't be her. She was a fool to even dream it. If three years of therapy hadn't solved her problem, how could a night with Ethan Cowan?

Naomi bit back the fear, the caustic anger at the unfairness of it, and plastered a smile on her famous lips as his body moved closer …

THEY WERE ALONE in the elevator. Hell, one of his biggest fantasies involved fucking Naomi in an elevator.

Ethan stared at the doors as they closed, hyperaware of the rapid rise and fall of her breasts as she stood next to him. A couple of times earlier he'd noticed her erect nipples under the gold fabric of her dress, and he'd gone hard in nanoseconds.

All through the event, he'd been fighting a war with his erection. Now, he had to cover his crotch with his hands, and thank Christ they were big because they only just covered his engorged dick.

He stifled a groan. Spending these last few hours with Naomi, infinitely close but not able to touch, hold, nuzzle, suck and thrust into her, was driving him insane.

Ethan cleared his throat and stared up at the mirrored ceiling. The sight of Naomi's incredible cleavage below the styled crown of her head hit him smack between the eyes.

Shit. Clearly nowhere was safe.

With all his fame, the continual flow of women hurling themselves at him, it was *that one* memory that filled his every fantasy. It was Naomi he longed for, and yet he'd never dared ask her out for anything more than a casual lunch.

She was completely out of his league, and his tongue tied in knots every time he saw her.

It was white-hot lust, sure, but also so much more than that. He admired her beyond words. A self-made woman, building her business with no help from her mega-wealthy shite of a dad. He'd learnt from Luke what an arsehole their father had been to her, how he put her down with malice that bordered on verbal abuse. It made Ethan's blood boil. He'd almost cheered when the old bastard died last year, glad that Naomi could escape that level of cruelty. It wasn't a coincidence, Ethan guessed, that the money from the NAO-ME masked ball was going to women's refuges.

The elevator was moving now and Ethan shuffled his feet, trying to think of something to say. Fucking embarrassing, his whole body lighting up like the Olympic flame whenever she glanced his way.

She spoke first. 'Thanks for accompanying me tonight. It really meant a lot.' Naomi had incredible stage presence, but now her voice was unbearably vulnerable.

He flicked her a glance. Her head bent, he let his gaze rest for a split second on the line of her neck descending into the creamy perfection of her left breast.

'Pleasure.' He sounded gruff. 'Anytime.'

'Anytime? Really?'

'Sure. I'm your man.'

She laughed huskily, which did nothing for his equilibrium. 'Mmm, my very own personal escort. I might take you up on that.'

The lift dinged before he could form words. Their rooms were on the same floor. Ethan stood back to let her go first, trying not to let his eyes stray to her beautiful butt as she walked.

They halted at her door. She searched for her key card in her purse, and maybe he was standing too close because as she turned, she gave a sudden jolt and swayed into him.

'Woah.' He reached out to steady her.

Her eyes flew to his face and it struck him how neither of them had thought to remove their masks.

He should step away, but something about her eyes and mouth made him step closer, daring to reach up and trace the pad of his thumb along the delicate line of her jaw. Her lips parted, her breasts rose sharply with an intake of breath.

'Can I kiss you goodnight?' he whispered.

She hesitated. 'I …'

'Just say the word and I'll stop.'

'Oh, I … want … but, no, I … I can't.'

'Am I treading on another guy's toes?'

She let out a desperate little mewl. 'No. There's no one, it's not like that at all. I …'

He kept stroking her jaw, his cock pressed hard and painful against his fly. Ethan gritted his teeth. No way would he overstep the mark.

Voices coming down the corridor kicked Naomi's head up. She brought out her key card, swiped it and before he knew it, had dragged him inside and shut the door.

For a second, they stood frozen in the darkness. Hesitantly, he lifted his hands and placed them gently on her shoulders. City lights shining through the expanse of the window gradually illuminated her face—beautiful yet gaunt, like a hunted animal.

'Naomi,' he whispered.

'Ethan.'

'I want to make love to you.' Again, his voice was barely more than a whisper.

She moaned, took a step toward him and laid her head against his chest. He reached up and stroked the soft coil of her hair.

She seemed close to sobbing. 'I can't. I mean, I can, but I can't …'

'Tell me.'

'I—oh God.' She rasped in a breath, exhaled. 'I don't have sex with men anymore.'

Was she gay? That could be it, and yet he knew she'd had a string of boyfriends. Maybe she went both ways. Ethan hesitated, not sure what to say and she filled the gap.

'This is *so* awkward. I—I've been in therapy. I've never …'

He felt her body shift against him.

'Shit, I really can't believe I'm telling you this.'

'It's ok, you could never shock me,' he urged gently.

He felt every muscle in her body brace. 'I've never had an orgasm. With a guy, that is.'

'Or with a woman?' he asked, desperate to know if he had a chance with her.

Her laugh was brittle. 'Hah, probably should try it, but no. Not with a woman, either. I've chosen not to fake it anymore. Years and years of pretending. Of never being able to, you know, let go … never feeling … loved enough I guess. So I don't. Have sex. Anymore.'

'But, are you able to … orgasm?' He couldn't help the question flying out of his mouth and held his breath. Was Naomi going to lie to him?

'Yes, on my own.' She whispered.

Silence vibrated in the darkness while he held her and tried to control his own body's reaction to her.

Naomi let out another shuddering sigh and then, barely audible, said, 'I think of you. When I … when I—'

'Come?'

'Uh-uh.' Her head hung low.

Ethan expelled a breath as his cock bucked harder. This had to be the most beautiful, sexy admission ever. He nuzzled his lips into her hair, around her ear, and breathed softly, 'What do you imagine doing with me?'

She let out a gasp, rolling her neck against his mouth. 'You. Touching me.'

'Where?'

'My breasts, thighs, my … my clit.'

'How do I touch your clit?'

'Soft circles, then firmer. Faster.'

'Show me.'

'Oh no! I mean, I couldn't. You must find me disgusting.'

Daringly, he rolled his aching, swollen crotch into her pelvis. 'Does it *feel* like I'm disgusted?'

She groaned and pushed her hips into him. Ethan bit his lower lip hard and stared at the city lights over her head to stop himself coming on the spot.

'We'll keep our masks on. We won't turn on the lights.' His voice sounded alien, deep and guttural with desire. 'We can lie on the bed, and you do what you do when you imagine I'm …' He layered soft kisses down the line of her neck and she stretched like a kitten into him, whimpering softly.

'Oh God, no. I really can't.'

'Hey, shh, shh, there are no rules here. It's just you and

me, Naomi. You can do anything you want to, anything you *need* to. And I won't touch you unless you ask me to.'

God, if only she knew how long he'd waited.

She gave a nod and he twined her fingers in his and led her towards the bed. They sat next to each other and Ethan tried to fathom what to do next. She had to take the lead, he couldn't, wouldn't.

Suddenly, she placed a palm on his cheek, leaned in and kissed him, her other hand ripping at his shirt buttons, lips hot and demanding, her tongue forking into his mouth nearly driving him past his limits.

He used every tactic of his game to hold back, every psychological strategy he'd ever learned, both on and off the field.

'Can I undress you?' he gasped against her mouth.

She pulled back and nodded again. Slowly, he pushed down her shoulder straps, feathering kisses over the surge of her cleavage but not going lower. She stood and he peeled down her dress until it pooled on the ground. Laying his head against the soft dome of her belly, Ethan breathed in the sweet scent of her, the subtler undertone of desire. He sensed Naomi reach up and undo her bra, and looking up, he saw the release of her perfect breasts, the upturn of her dusky nipples, just like he remembered.

Ethan heard himself groan, but he muted it. Her fingers tangled in his hair as she pressed his head against her stomach. He dared to plant a row of kisses above the line of silk and lace that hid her sweet pussy, let his hands circle her and rest gently on the cheeks of her butt.

She whimpered softly. He knew that sound and his cock knew it, too. Surely his skin couldn't stretch over its swollen length for much longer?

'Show me,' he murmured, gazing up at her parted lips,

those amazing eyes, dark and sultry behind the mask. 'Lie down and show me.'

For a moment, he felt her shrink away, but he held her steady. 'Show me, Naomi. I want to know how to please you.'

With a sigh, she folded onto the bed, shimmied up the length of it and he joined her cautiously, lying beside her, head resting on his hand, not too close. Not touching. Still dressed.

'Take your clothes off,' she demanded.

He needed no prompting. Through her mask, he could tell her eyes were hungry as he stood and ripped off everything. Her gaze trailed a line of fire down his body until it reached the rigid jut of his cock and she gasped. He was burning up for her, fast running out of orbit.

'Oh my God, you're magnificent.'

Naomi licked her lips as he knelt on his haunches on the bed. Without breaking eye contact, she pushed down her panties. She arched her hips and spread-eagled her thighs. Nestled in her pink cleft and dusting of blonde hair, the bud of her clit glistened like some ridiculously precious jewel as her fingers swooped and swirled, then dipped inside her entrance, and back. Her other hand found its way to her nipple, pinching and kneading, and the whole time her eyes were fixed on his cock.

'Touch yourself,' she begged.

'Fuck, I want you.' It came out a harsh growl. He'd meant to contain it, not to push her past what she was ready for, but now with his fist jerking his cock as he knelt over her, seeing her laid out below him, Ethan couldn't hold back the jumble of longing falling from his mouth.

'So much, Naomi. Wanted you forever, since I—*Jesus Christ*, look at your beautiful breasts, your clit. I—'

'Yesss, keep talking.' Naomi's head thrashed, her hair unravelling as her hand danced over her sex.

He let the words spill out, everything he'd wanted to say for years, all the pent-up desire he'd held back for so long.

He could tell she was getting close, the muscles of her thighs tensing, toes flexing.

She cried out. 'Come with me, Ethan!'

'You want me to?'

'Yes, yes, I want to see you, feel you come on me.'

'Tell me when.'

He devoured the sight of her—sweat sheening her brow, her eyes feverish behind the satin of her mask, teeth biting her lower lip. Her movements quickened. Their gazes locked as he shifted over her belly, their panting breath in unison.

'Oh *Jesus*! Now! Ethan, now!' She screamed, her body bunching beneath him, head arching back.

That was all it took. With a guttural cry of release, he came ferociously in long spumes, falling into her universe as Naomi called his name over and over and shuddered beneath him.

NAOMI WANTED TO PINCH HERSELF. Had this really happened? Her and Ethan, making passionate love through mutual self-pleasuring?

Floating down from the heights of her orgasm, she found herself giggling as Ethan held her close and kissed her eyelids. Everything was sticky, doused in the musky scent of his semen.

God, he'd nearly drowned them both.

'Why are you laughing?' Ethan's breath was still ragged as he rolled his forehead against hers.

'Oh, just because …'

Because this was the most amazing dream come true.

'Do you think we could take our masks off now?' He asked, his lips beneath it shaping a grin.

'You mean expose our faces after the best sex ever?' She couldn't help laughing again, feeling free for the first time in her life. 'Wouldn't that be a bit, um … intimate?'

Ethan kissed the tip of her nose. 'I think we could risk it.'

Naomi gave a mock pout. 'If you get the tissue box.'

A few minutes later, they were lying on their sides, gazing into each other's naked faces. Ethan's eyes luminous grey, the eyes she'd adored from that first day she met him.

He stared at her, studying every millimetre of her face as though she were *The Mona Lisa*. Two fingers trailed across her cheek and traced the outline of her mouth, slow and achingly sweet. She nipped them with her lips, let her tongue flick across them, salty from his semen

The hungry jut of his cock told her he was ready for more. Like *now*.

'You know, with you, I think I could learn to let go … if we had more time together …'

His arms tightened around her. 'God, Naomi, you've had all of me from the moment I first saw you.'

Her heart did a crazy somersault. 'When you came home with Luke all those years ago, I fell for you big time. But you were crazy shy, you wouldn't look at me all weekend.'

He stayed silent and she thought she'd said something wrong.

'That wasn't the first time I… met you." he said at last.

'Don't be silly, I would remember.'

His chest expanded on a sharp intake of breath. 'Naomi, if we're going to see more of each other, become a couple—which God knows I want more than anything— I have to come clean about something.'

Couple? He wanted that as much as she did? Her heart pumped even more wildly, but … *Come clean?* Confusion held her back.

'You were in the bathroom,' he said quietly.

'Bathroom?'

'Yes, I nearly walked in on you the night I arrived. You were … touching yourself.'

'Oh my God, no! You saw me *masturbating?*'

She tried to pull away, but his arms maintained their gentle hold.

'Hear me out, *please*, Naomi. You were the most beautiful girl I'd ever seen, and I … I couldn't stop myself. Oh shit, now it's my turn to find this really fucking difficult. I came. With you. Outside the door.' His features contorted, eyes blazing. 'It was the best orgasm I've ever had. Until tonight.'

Naomi didn't know whether to laugh or cry. All this time she'd fantasised about Ethan without knowing *this*. She should be horrified, but as she gazed into his face, all she saw was love.

And yes, she loved this guy, too. Those times he'd taken her for coffee or lunch, the blood had fizzed in her veins at the way his eyes devoured her. How could she blame him? He'd seen her in her most abandoned state and wanted her. There was nothing more to hide.

A surge of unbelievable happiness pulsed through her. 'You're kidding. You and I had a simultaneous orgasm and I never knew about it?'

He nodded.

'Though, I did wonder what all the streaks on the

carpet were the next morning.' Somehow, she kept a straight face.

His face fell. 'Shit, really?

Relenting, Naomi rubbed her nose into Ethan's neck, it smelt deliciously of his cologne and them. 'No, of course not.'

He gave a sigh of relief. 'Do you forgive me?'

She kissed his mouth, ran her tongue along the seam of his lips and felt his immediate spasm of desire.

'How could I not when I was your first pin-up girl?'

'And my last.'

She reached for Ethan's hand and placed his fingers with hers on her pulsing clit.

'I think it's time for lesson number two,' she murmured.

'I'm ready, lover.'

Taking a Chance

WL DAVIES

ALICE BENTON STRUGGLED to maintain her professional facade as she watched zombies and centaurs get it on with fairies and cowgirls. She'd had no choice about attending the company's costume party, but how anyone could think wearing a mask was an effective disguise was unfathomable. She'd been working with these people for less than two months and could identify everyone.

But for tonight, her colleagues seemed happy wearing costumes that had no bearing on their usual personalities. Including her.

She glanced towards Zorro leaning against the wall, partly obscured by a support beam and the dull lighting. Dressed all in black, his shirt and trousers fitted him like a second skin. The cloak thrown over his broad shoulders outlined his fit and lean body perfectly. His black, broad-brimmed hat was tilted at a jaunty angle, the sword on his hip looked authentic. His dark mask, which made his blue eyes even more alluring, gave him a slightly dangerous but very intriguing air. Blue eyes that studied her with calm appraisal, sending warmth through her limbs.

She'd heard about Bryce Hunter's ability to turn the most mundane idea into an awe-inspiring advertisement before she'd met him. A talented graphic artist, he'd won awards that boosted the company's reputation, but she'd never expected him to be so good-looking. Or that she'd be instantly attracted to him, regardless of how … inconvenient … that was.

She'd tried to ignore her attraction to him, but it had grown as the days and weeks went by. Thankfully, he worked in a different building, so she could avoid him when things got too … uncomfortable. Yes, he was handsome. Yes, he was a dedicated employee, and he had a wicked sense of humour.

But she'd never cross the line, no matter what her heart said. Or how many times she'd been tempted to give in and let her feelings rule, despite the consequences. Indeed, she had no right to be standing there, practically drooling over the darkly dressed man standing in the shadows.

Alice stiffened slightly, reaching to adjust her mask, ensuring it was still in place. Zorro hadn't taken his eyes from her, not once. She should have turned away. She should have ignored him, but as he approached, she was unable, and unwilling, to avert her gaze. Those intense blue eyes held hers, trapping her.

'Alice.'

One word was all it took. Her throat tightened as she played with the red ties that held her dress together. The tone of his voice, the way he said her name, sent shivers up and down her spine.

'Bryce,' she murmured in response.

'Would you like to dance?' He held his hand out to her as the opening bars of a slow ballad began.

After their first dance together she'd been categorically told by higher management how inappropriate and unprofessional her actions were. Dancing with him tonight would not be sensible, even though every atom of her being was straining towards him, longing to be in his arms once more.

'I don't think that's a good idea.'

'Probably not,' he replied. She let out a breath she hadn't realised she'd held. 'But let's see if our dance at the awards dinner was as good as I remember.' He gave her his trademark grin. The one that made her resolve weaken and her heart rate increase. 'Let's see if we *are* good partners. What do you say?'

If she closed her eyes, she could still feel his arms around her, the heat of his body moving with hers as they'd danced together. He'd held her steady, his warm hands clasped in hers, sending thrills all the way through her as he'd spun her out and pulled her back towards him. She'd felt like she'd been floating on air. The moment they'd looked into each other's eyes as the music surrounded them was something she'd remember forever.

She hesitated for another moment. 'Oh-kay.'

'Thank you,' he whispered, sending shivers down her spine.

Bryce's warm hand enclosed hers. His grip tightened as he gently tugged her towards him, his strong arms surrounding her, his woody scent making her dizzy. They began moving, dancing as if they'd been partners for years. He was so close, the heat from his body sent waves of electricity through her. Her heart was pounding so hard it was a wonder he couldn't hear it. Her breathing grew shallow as she concentrated on moving smoothly and fluently.

'You know, I'm not someone who gives up easily,' he said, his voice husky and low. 'I'm hoping you'll feel our connection, as deeply as me.' The hint of his breath against her cheek caused goose bumps to erupt all over her.

'Be assured, I'd do anything for you.' His expression was entirely serious. 'Anything.'

She sighed, melting into his embrace, the entire world fading away but for the two of them.

An eternity later, the song ended, but they remained on the dance floor, staring into each other's eyes. The next song was already halfway through when Bryce led her towards the darkened corner he'd been standing in prior to their dance.

'I hope you know that the main reason I'm leaving is so we can have a chance. Together.'

'Wait,' she said, her head spinning. 'Did you just say you're leaving?'

'Yeah. I'm starting my own business. Well, that happened ages ago. But now I have more work than I can cope with. So, something had to give.'

His blue eyes connected with hers, full of warmth and just a glint of excitement too. '*This* job was that something.'

'Congratulations,' she said, 'I'm sure you'll be very successful.'

She spread her hands out over her chest, her posture automatically going rigid. Bryce leaving could mean …

No, she wouldn't start spinning dream-like threads of happy-ever-afters with him. Not when she still wasn't convinced her own position was secure. Besides, the timing was a bit suspicious, especially after the comments she'd received about their behaviour at the awards dinner. Was he being forced out, or was this a voluntary move on his part? And that ache in her heart had nothing to do with the realisation that they wouldn't be seeing each other regularly. Nor that she'd miss him.

He let out a short snicker. 'Well, the romance covers I design sure seem to be selling well.'

She frowned. 'Romance covers?' What the hell was he talking about?

'I've been designing romance book covers for a while now,' he continued, ignoring her gasp of surprise. 'They're fun to do, and some are even bestsellers.'

'That's … surprising,' she replied, her tone flat.

'What? You're not a fan of romance?'

'I …' She gulped, took a step back and crossed her arms. 'Romance doesn't exist, not in real life. It's a fantasy that little girls are fed for some stupid reason. It's …'

Too hurtful was what she wanted to say but refrained.

'Important,' he replied, his tone firm and decisive.

Her lips parted and her body trembled slightly at the heated look in his eyes as they roamed over her costume, taking in her bare legs and lingering on her scantily covered torso.

'Let me tell you, red definitely looks good on you,' he continued after a small pause. 'I should have told you that right from the get-go, but I was too stunned by your beauty to get my mouth and brain to work in tandem.'

It was her turn to let out a short snigger. 'Go on,' she said, 'you've got my attention.'

'I'm really glad you came as Little Red Riding Hood,' he replied, his eyes once more scanning her costume, sending bolts of lightning straight to her core.

'I'm loving the way your red cape falls off your shoulders like that. It draws my eye to your glossy brown hair.' His eyes darkened, and his hand came up to gently push a strand behind her ear.

'And that silver broach is tempting me to unclasp your cape and let it fall to the ground.'

'So, you're being the big bad wolf in the fairy tale now? Trying to convince me you really are my grandmother? Trying to persuade me to come inside?'

He frowned. 'Maybe I'll have to lift my game.'

'Oh, this is going to be good,' she replied, not trying to hide her sarcasm.

He took his time, looking at her as if he really saw her, the person she was inside and not the professional she portrayed to the world.

'I've always loved your green eyes,' he said after a long, heated moment. 'And your mask makes them even more interesting. Indeed, when I gaze into their gorgeous depths, I lose all sense of where I am.'

He moved closer until his body heat enveloped her, making her lips part on a silent sigh. Her fingers tingled with the need to reach out and caress him. To run her hands down his arms and over his chest. To outline his lips with her fingertips. To run her tongue over his exception-ally kissable mouth. She'd love to strip him of his dark costume, including his mask, so they could stand in front of each other, visible and free.

'And that dress you've got on underneath your cloak is distracting.' He grinned. 'It showcases your curves beau-tifully.'

He looked around the room as warmth flooded her.

'I'm sure most of the guys have thought about hitting on you. But seeing as you're one promotion away from senior management, it looks like I'm the only one brave enough to approach you. Besides, those guys still need their jobs come Monday.'

She felt her skin flush and she became more aware of her own heartbeat than ever before. It thundered away like a loud percussion instrument. She licked her dry lips.

'Oh, come on, that's bullshit. And you know it,' she said, her tone weaker than she'd intended it to be.

'Nope, it's the truth.'

'And what, you've nothing to fear now that you're leaving?'

'Not a damn thing,' he agreed, his mouth twitching. 'To me, you're worth coming out of the shadows for.' His blue eyes looked deep into hers, making her breath hitch and her panties damp.

'I am?'

What was with her? She was an intelligent, well-respected woman, but here she was acting like some sort of horny teenager on her first date. Alice tried to stand straighter, but that just brought Bryce's amazing body closer.

'Now, if we're talking romance …'

His voice was so low, she had to tilt her head to hear him properly. Sparks erupted, their heated connection growing into something stronger, something much more substantial.

'… that'll mean doing something I've been longing to do.'

'What's that?'

'Kissing you.'

He leaned in until his hard chest rested against the clasp of the cloak. It felt wonderful and exciting. Her breathing grew more rapid, and her hands twitched. It took almost everything she had not to reach up and knock his hat off his head so she could tangle her hands through his blond hair.

'In my fantasies our kiss starts out slow and gentle,' he continued quietly, 'your lips soft and pliant against mine. Then you gasp, leaving a small gap that allows our tongues to tangle together.'

Her breathing was so shallow and fast that dark spots appeared at the edge of her vision. But nothing could make her move away. It was like she was hypnotised, held captive by the tale he told her. Her nerves fired and heat swamped her.

'You've given this a lot of thought,' she whispered.

He nodded. 'You're so beautiful,' he breathed, his eyes showing his sincerity. 'Before long, we'll be kissing so deeply, we'll both be trembling with need.' He gave her a look that pierced straight through to her heart.

'But …' She blinked, trying to clear the fog that surrounded her brain. She tried to move back but remained frozen in place. 'No, that's not going to happen.' She stood straighter. 'You might be leaving, but I'm not. I still need to maintain my reputation within this company.'

'Us seeing each other, having a relationship, has nothing to do with your job,' he replied, frowning. He took a breath. 'Is this why you've been avoiding me? You think I'm out to ruin your career?'

'You want a relationship?'

He let out a grunt. 'Yes, of course I want a relationship with you, Alice. We're good together. We have chemistry. We're both ambitious. We share the same sense of humour and have the same outlook on life.'

He speared her with his blue eyes once more.

'It's not me who's been denying our connection.' He sighed, his breath sending shivers over her skin. 'But I guess I can understand your … reluctance … to get involved.'

'So, you haven't been pushed out?'

He raised his chin and shook his head.

'Or made to feel like you have to leave for any reason?'

'Not at all.' He paused, looking directly into her eyes. 'I'm leaving because the timing's right. It's what I want to do with my life. It's something I've been planning for longer than I've known you.'

'So, you didn't come dressed like that—,' she deliberately ran her eyes up and down his body, lingering a bit too long on his chest and his thighs, '—just to make me swoon at your feet like some lovesick heroine?'

She knew her words were sharp and harsh. She'd done what she always did whenever anyone came too close — got defensive. Her body shook with the emotion he'd churned up inside, the longing she'd suppressed for too long. All that denial, ignoring her needs, was coming to the fore. Now. Tonight. And she couldn't do a single thing about it.

'Swoon?' he said, his eyes gleaming in amusement. 'And you said you didn't believe in romance.'

She stood there and stared at him.

'As for the Zorro outfit,' he continued, 'I actually wanted to come as Superman.'

Two people dressed as Superman walked past. One slightly overweight, the other too old to pull the outfit off convincingly.

'I thought it was the perfect way to breakout of the Clark Kent persona everyone's labelled me with.' His lips twitched. 'But luckily I'm the only Zorro here.'

He took a step back, flinging his arms out, making his black cape swirl. He turned, drawing his sword in what looked like practised fluidity, his blue eyes gleaming from behind his mask.

'My sword is at your disposal, ready for you to command.' He held the sword up in a Zorro-like pose. 'Ready to satisfy your needs, if that's my lady's wish.'

He lowered the sword, tip pointing to the ground. He moved his other hand in a wide circular motion before executing an elaborate bow, making her heart melt and her heated cheeks glow.

He straightened and looked around the room again.

'Let's get out of here,' he said, resetting his sword effortlessly. 'To somewhere … more private.'

'You mean back to your place?'

He shrugged. 'If you like.'

'Or were you expecting me to ask you back to mine?'

His hands travelled down the front of his pants, drawing her attention to his thighs. His pants were so tight, every muscle outlined, they made her mouth moisten with need. How she'd love to wrap her legs around those thighs as he filled her, thrusting into her, making her scream.

'How about we go grab a coffee somewhere?'

He looked both pleading and determined at the same time.

How did he do that? How did he manage to break down her barriers so easily? Alice shook, trying to remember that having a fling with Bryce was disastrous for her career. No matter how much her heart, and her body, wanted that very thing.

'Forget coffee. Let's go to my place.'

He looked as stunned as she felt, hardly able to believe those words had come flying, unbidden, from her mouth.

'Okay,' he replied, his tone confident, eager, with no hesitation whatsoever.

THEY ENDED up at his place.

As soon as they left the party, Alice realised what a spectacle they presented. She was dressed as Little Red Riding Hood. He was the sexiest Zorro she'd ever seen. And the taxi beeping its horn as it went past with a feminine 'hey handsome' comment thrown out the window was enough to bring home that fact.

His apartment wasn't as big as hers. A room immedi

ately off the entryway they stood in looked to be the lounge room—because what else could it be? It had two two-seater couches joined together to make a corner unit with a coffee table between. A small kitchen was off the corridor, which probably lead to his bedroom. A place she'd longed to visit, but never thought she would.

Everything was as neat and tidy as his desk at work.

He took off his cloak and hung it on the stand inside the door. His sword and hat came off next, but his mask stayed on.

They both removed their shoes.

Her heels sitting neatly beside his black boots unnerved her, sending thoughts of what it would be like living with him flying through her head. Thoughts that had no place being aired tonight. This wasn't about that. It was a one-time thing, an outlet. A way to tamper her crazy attraction, to get things out of her system and her life back to normal. She'd be stupid to hope for anything more.

Before she could drag her eyes off their footwear, he'd unclasped the silver broach holding her red cape together. His fingers caressed her as he slowly removed it from around her shoulders. The blue of his eyes darkened, his expression warm and open as they stood close together, taking in the sight of each other.

'Let me get you that coffee,' he said, his tone husky, indicating she should move into the lounge room.

'I don't want coffee.' She moved closer to him, closer even than when they'd danced. The heat of his body enveloped her, and her breath caught when his woody scent wafted over her. 'I want you.'

'I had hoped we could talk,' he said, his tone unsure, 'but maybe we'll put that off,' he placed his hands around her waist, 'until later?'

'Excellent choice,' she replied, leaning in towards him,

her eyes centred on his lips. His scent drove her crazy, making her need to get as close to him as possible skyrocket.

He moved her until her back was pressed against the apartment door. His arms wound around her. His whole body pressed against hers. He looked into her eyes for a long, heart-pounding minute. She wrapped her foot around the back of his knee, pressing her body closer. His hands shifted from her waist to her hips, sending bolts of pleasure and warmth through her.

'Alice,' he groaned, his tone huskier than before.

She leaned forward and placed her lips against his.

He reacted instantly, licking the seam of her lips with the tip of his tongue, encouraging her to let him in. She did so without hesitation, their tongues dancing together, mimicking the way their bodies moved. He tasted so good, better than she'd dreamed he would.

His hardness was obvious, and she took great delight in rubbing herself over him, soaking her underwear and making her desire spin out of control. He pulled her more firmly against his length and she moaned.

'You're so beautiful,' he said, the words coming out like a long groan. 'You feel so good.'

She wanted to tell him he felt even better. She wanted to say how wonderful it felt to have his hard cock stroking her, even while still clothed. How the reality of being there with him was better than anything she could imagine. That she'd give him anything he wanted if only he continued to hold her close, allowing her to move against him, ratcheting up the intensity of their connection.

'We should probably slow down.' He gasped, his breathing ragged, his eyes blazing.

'Slowing down is the last thing we should do.'

Despite his lean body, he didn't have any trouble

keeping her plastered against the door, her toes barely touching the ground. He leaned back slightly, the better to look at her.

'You don't want to discuss where this is going?'

'No.' She knew, or at least she hoped she knew, exactly where this was going.

'Okay,' he replied, 'but I'm not going to take you against the door to my apartment.' He grinned. 'Not our first time, anyway.'

She giggled; something she rarely did.

He took her hand and led her into the lounge room, not towards his bedroom as she expected. He wrapped his arms around her again, sending tingles and desire racing through her body. She wanted to crawl all over him. To press kisses all over his body until he couldn't take it anymore. She wanted him to lose control, completely.

'Are you sure this is what you want Alice?'

'Absolutely,' she replied.

'You know I want you,' he said, taking a deep breath. 'That much is obvious.' He rested his head against her. 'But I want more than a quick roll in the sack.'

He separated them, but only just. Still, he may as well as moved to the other side of the room.

'I want you. All of you. I want us to date. To be together as a couple.'

He stared at her, his eyes spearing her as they had at the party. She barely controlled her trembling muscles, her heart thundering away like a bass drum inside her chest. All thoughts of her career, the opinions of upper manage-ment, everything was swept away because of the desire she saw reflected in his eyes.

'I would never do anything that would deliberately hurt or humiliate you. If you have any doubts about us, tell me now.'

She didn't respond.

Instead, she captured his lips, ceasing further discussion.

Her need for him was too overwhelming. He kissed her back eagerly, deeply. She drank in his taste, longing for them to be joined, fully. She didn't care about anything but him. She increased the heat of their kiss until they had to break apart, breathing hard.

'Need—you,' she gasped.

'You've got me,' he responded, 'heart and soul.'

He removed her mask slowly, setting it on top of the coffee table.

She immediately felt vulnerable, exposed. Taking a deep breath, revelling in his woody scent, she ignored that fission of fear and concentrated on what she wanted. Him.

She unbuttoned his black shirt, slowly revealing his chest. She ran her hands up and over his muscles, playing with the blond hair that lightly covered him. His own hands roamed her body in a knee-weakening exploration that left her barely able to stand. One hand snaked up her bare leg to her upper thigh, under the short skirt of her costume, sending jolts of erotic sensation through her. After a minute, he moved both hands towards the ties below her breast, loosening her black and red dress, leaving the white top gaping open.

She leaned forward and pressed her lips against his nipple, causing him to squirm and groan as she sucked hard. His hands travelled into her hair, and he ran the strands through his fingers in a gentle, languid motion.

She moved away slightly and watched him, sighing when he caught her lips in a searing kiss. After long, heated minutes, they broke apart, breathing hard.

'Alice.'

Her name escaped his lips on a groan. One that

expressed a deep well of desire and longing. She reached around and undid his mask, revealing his handsome face at last. It felt momentous, removing it, like she was uncovering the man behind it in all his complexity. But she didn't have long to contemplate this insight because he kissed her again, hotter and deeper than before.

She reached for his pants, unbuttoning them and pushing them down his legs. His hands wandered to her hips, the feel of them sending her heart soaring. He peeled her dress off her, leaving her in her bra and panties. He studied her closely, his eyes going an even darker blue, his breathing laboured, his erection obvious, making her mouth water.

He flopped onto the couch in his underwear, pulling her onto his lap. His hands immediately went to her breasts, caressing and squeezing them, driving her crazy.

'You're amazing.'

He unhooked her bra, flinging it across the room before taking one nipple in his mouth, rolling it between his lips and biting gently.

She gasped and arched her back, allowing him better access. She delighted in showing him exactly how good this felt, grinding against his cock in a way that made her desire grow into an inferno. She took deep, steadying breaths, surrounding herself in their combined scent. Everything about him turned her on.

'Naked,' he said.

The order made her smile. She'd caused him to descend into single-word sentences, and the satisfaction that brought increased her need for him enormously.

She shimmied out of her knickers, allowing them to fall to the ground. She displayed her body for Bryce's inspection and his eyes devoured her, heating her skin.

'Your turn,' she said, her tone husky.

He complied with alacrity, stripping his boxers off so fast it was almost comical. She pushed him back onto the couch and straddled him.

She watched him watching her as she moved her body in a slow, deliberate way that drove them both crazy. Crazy good. His hands curved over her breasts, caressing her, sending waves of pleasure straight to her core.

'Alice,' he said in a strangled voice. 'I need to be inside you.'

She grinned at him. 'So, what's stopping you?'

He reached between them and guided himself inside her. Her head fell back at the sheer pleasure of being filled by him. He kissed her jaw and throat as he pushed in and out.

'Alice,' he said, his lips nuzzling her neck.

The tip of his tongue flicked against her racing pulse. He gripped her hips tightly, moving her in a rhythm that made her moan loudly. She continued to sway back and forth, setting a cadence that satisfied them both.

He thrust in and out, responding to her sighs and her moans. He increased his thrusts, then backed off slightly, altering their tempo and the angle of his plunges, sending her spiralling toward orgasm.

'Yes, just like that,' she groaned.

Leaning forward, he took one of her nipples in his mouth, sliding his tongue over it, sucking gently.

'More,' she gasped.

Hot. Intense. Perfect. He hit that magic spot inside, making her buck and writhe frenetically. Their connection, the feel of him, was like nothing she'd ever experienced. She exploded, her orgasm hitting her so hard she nearly blacked out. He let out a deep, long groan as he erupted inside her a second later.

She felt shaky, shocked at their intimacy and how

magnificent he was. At the way he'd encouraged her to be as wild as she wanted. How he'd cherished her sexual abandonment and revelled in their lovemaking. And she'd delighted in his gentleness, at the way he'd accepted her. All of her, not just the professional persona she showed the world, but the woman she was deep inside.

All her concerns about having a relationship with Bryce, about how it would impact her career and her heart, melted into insignificance.

Before tonight, she'd been scared. Too scared to be her authentic self. Now, she didn't care what anyone thought. Not the senior executives, not anyone. And now she finally understood the term "making love", because that's just what they'd done.

They touched foreheads, staring into each other's eyes, breathing hard as they both recovered. She moved off him, grabbing his black shirt and dragging it over her head. He retrieved his pants and pulled them on before sitting down next to her. He smiled and captured her lips in his once more.

'Can we talk about our future now?'

'I—'

'I think about you, day and night,' he said, his tone serious, his eyes pleading. 'From the minute I wake to when I go to sleep.'

He turned that gorgeous grin of his towards her, causing her heart rate to accelerate after it had only just returned to something approaching normal.

'And then you come to me in my dreams.'

'I'm sure we can work something out,' she replied, her tone exactly like what she used in the boardroom.

His eyes twinkled, and his mouth twitched.

Alice knew the benefit of silence when negotiating important deals. She used that skill now, taking her time, looking him in the eye, hoping she kept the rising excitement and anticipation from her expression.

'I guess I can take a chance on you.' She grinned. 'As long as we get to make love again, I'll happily be yours. Exclusively.'

'At last,' he said, swooping in and kissing her until she forgot everything but him.

A Mask for Carnevale

SHANNON SLIQUE

'*BUONGIORNO CARA*. It is time to lose the mask, no? Here in Venice, it's a night-time thing. Not even for Carnevale do we wear the mask in bed—usually.'

The rich, molten tones washed over Chelsea's morning sleepiness as a feather drifted up her leg and over her stomach—her naked stomach—and on to her breasts.

'After such a night as ours, you don't need to be coy. I want to see you. I demand to know you. More than just your delightful body.'

Lips descended onto Chelsea's breast and a hand replaced the feather. It smoothed its way over the rounded features of her body without pause, and arrowed into the narrow strip of hair that accorded a small disguise to her intimate space. The auburn curls were no barrier, and two fingers slipped inside without hesitation. Her body jerked in response.

'*Bella.*' He inhaled the scent between her breasts. '*Bella*, you are already hot and waiting for me. Let me know that you want me inside you.'

Chelsea raised a languid hand and dragged his face

from her chest. She fisted her fingers in his hair to anchor his mouth to hers. His nose pressed the lower edge of her mask into her skin, but she ignored the discomfort.

She stabbed her tongue into his mouth and tasted brandy and leftover lust. Her tongue roamed over his, exploring the roughness of it and sliding along the central crevice.

His cock grew harder where it lay against her hip. She reached one hand down to stroke it and found it already sheathed.

Her other hand slid from his thick, curly, dark hair to cup his cheek, and she opened her eyes to feast on his features. God, he was beautiful. He could have been the model for Michelangelo's *David*. Her eyes snagged his and she smiled. Her body ached in all the right places, but she wasn't going to let her last opportunity to be with this man pass her by.

'*Si signore*. Fuck me good.'

The nostrils of his aquiline nose flared, his face taut with desire.

He flexed his fingers inside her before pulling them out to nip her clitoris. Her body arched on a groan. All night, he'd played her body like a maestro, and he did it again now. Just one pluck at her clit and her body demanded its fulfilment.

He rose over her. '*Cara*, what an invitation!'

In one swift move, his cock rocketed into her canal and his balls slapped against her. He held still a moment and then set up a rhythmic pumping. His covered penis rasped against her tender clit and his balls massaged her perineum. Her tension rose higher. She couldn't control the pulse of her internal muscles. Still, he pumped. Slide, thrust! Slide, thrust!

Chelsea's head thrashed against the pillow and her

hands gripped the underside of the bedhead. A keening wail began deep in her chest and her heels rose higher up his back.

One pump more, two, and the cry erupted from her throat as he went into rigour and their bodies, together, found the peak of perfection they had been seeking. He held still above her as though suspended on the wave of passion and she savoured the moment.

He flopped onto the bed beside her, pulling her around to face him. '*Bella,* you are perfection in a bottle.' His eyes drifted closed.

Chelsea smiled at his comment. That was exactly what she thought of him.

She was tempted to snuggle down beside him and drift off, too. Instead, she watched him sleep for several minutes then slipped from the bed, gathered her small tote and her clothes, and closed herself in the spacious ensuite.

The accoutrements of the bathroom reflected the magnificence of the rest of the hotel. There were soft fluffy towels, a roomy shower and a massive bath.

She cracked open the door and saw her lover sound asleep.

Great, a quick shower was in order.

She worked her way through the several ribbons that had kept her mask and mini-headdress in place. She wrapped the feathers around the face-piece to keep them in order and folded the lot into her tote, wound her long auburn hair into a makeshift bun and stepped into the shower.

She was drying herself when she heard movement in the bedroom. She scrambled into her clothes, grabbed her tote and eased the door ajar. Voices came from the adjoining sitting room.

She stood and listened while she sought a means of exit

from the bedroom that wouldn't require going past the two men.

Her lover spoke in English, but his visitor used Italian, something about a dinner party that evening with his wife.

'*Solo, tu e la tua grassoccia piccola scopamica Australiana.*' He laughed.

'How did you know about her?'

'We saw and heard you in the parlour when we came in.'

'Ah. Then you know she is not plump, Leo. She is well-rounded in all the right places—much better than the beanpoles and teaspoon-titties you used to date.'

Chelsea noted that while her lover defended her curves, he didn't correct the "little Australian fuck buddy" bit.

Her heart dropped. Sure, she'd come to Venice with the expectation that she would find a temporary lover and put the barbs from her ex-fiancé behind her, but she'd felt a connection with this guy. That magical whump had hit her in the chest as soon as he had spoken to her in the crowd. Even with his face half-covered with a simple black mask, she'd wanted to know more about him.

Well, she knew now. He was up himself just like the rest of the world's male population. Fuck buddy, indeed!

She refused to hang around to hear any more labels. She found another door just outside the bathroom and leaned down on the handle.

Emerging into a gallery off the main stairs, she hefted her tote and strode in that direction.

A middle-aged man in a suit and top hat moved across the large entry foyer. He stopped and waited as she descended to his level.

'*Buongiorno signorina.*'

'*Buongiorno, lei parla inglese?*' She didn't want to struggle with Italian if this bloke could speak her own language.

'Certainly, miss. How can I help you?'

'You're English.'

'I am, and you're Australian.'

'Right.' She smiled. 'Could you point me in the direction of the Rialto, please?'

'I can, but it's below freezing out there this morning. Do you have a warmer jacket?'

'Nope, this is it. It didn't seem to be that cold last night.'

'Give me a moment.' He walked over to a large closet in the hallway and retrieved a long black coat. 'We keep these for emergencies. You can return it next time you're here.'

'Hmm, I'm not planning a next time, but if you write down the address of this place, I'll get the coat back to you.'

'Certainly, miss.' He handed her a card which read *Palazzo Ducoletti* and its location.

'You work here? You're not a guest?'

'I'm the butler, miss.'

'Ah. Could you put your name there, too, so I know who to get the coat back to?'

She paused as he wrote, then glanced again at the card and saw he had added "Butterworth".

'The Rialto?' she prompted.

'I'll take you to where you can easily find your way,' he offered.

Chelsea shrugged into the coat and trailed behind the butler. They went out a side entry that was out of sight of the *piazza* she had seen from the bedroom window. That had to be a good thing, right?

They exited directly onto a bridge crossing the canal. A speedboat was moored to one side at a jetty, much like a car would be parked, waiting, at home.

Butterworth led her through labyrinthine alleyways until he stopped at a corner. Chelsea was grateful for the woollen warmth of the coat. The air was damp and very cold.

'If you follow this walkway as it curves around and then go straight ahead, you'll see the Rialto Bridge a couple of hundred metres further on. Do you think you can manage?'

'Yes. Thanks, er, Butterworth.' She stopped and screwed her face into a grimace. 'Sorry, I just can't do that, call you by your surname. What comes before the Butterworth bit?'

A quick grin split the man's face. 'It's David, Miss.'

'David I can handle. Thanks for your help and I'm truly sorry for dragging you out into the cold.'

'It's my pleasure, Miss …?'

'Chelsea.' She held out her hand and he shook it. 'I'll get the coat back to you in the next couple of days. Thanks again.'

'Goodbye, Miss Chelsea.'

RAFAELE DUCOLLETTI SAT DRUMMING his fingers on the expanse of his desk, empty save for a newspaper. Work was a write-off. He couldn't take his mind off the woman who had sneaked out of his apartment yesterday.

It had been years since he'd let his guard down with a woman. On Saturday night, he'd gone for a stroll to take in the energy of Carnevale. It was a magical time in his city —the masks, the performers, the excitement. And there she had been, standing still and alone as the crowd of Piazza San Marco seethed around her. It had been as if she, too, were absorbing the atmosphere.

He'd had to meet her.

She'd smiled as he approached, and he'd felt like a dizzy schoolboy. He'd stuttered something about Carnevale and then asked if she'd like to have coffee or a drink with him.

As they finished their coffee, they'd followed it with a glass of prosecco, and another, and their conversation didn't falter.

They'd shared their first kiss when he passed her a gelato in the square. The kiss was like nothing he'd experienced before. Lightning energy spiked through his body, and he'd been lost in the moment. The nudge of someone passing by had pulled him back, but he'd wanted more.

They'd walked a while amid the crowd until they arrived at the door of his *palazzo*. She'd thought it was a hotel and he didn't disabuse her of that. It was, in a way, with the members of his family having their own suites of apartments scattered through it.

Butterworth had brought coffee and a selection of snacks. Raf had fed them to her as she sat beside him on the chaise longue. Her tongue had rasped against his fingertips and her eyes had darkened. He'd kissed her again, then. With no audience and no jostling crowd, it went on and on until their bodies had melted into each other.

That was when he'd invited her to stay. She'd hesitated a moment. He'd stood and held out his hand and she'd taken it.

What a night! Her Rubenesque figure delighted him. Her pillowy voluptuousness demanded his attention. His hands, mouth, tongue explored every morsel. He'd suckled her breasts and her clit in equal measure. She'd opened herself to him like no other lover had ever done. The only element she kept closed to him was the top half of her face —she wouldn't remove her mask.

Now, he slapped the desk in frustration and stood as his cousin Marco strolled into the office.

'What's up with you? Are you still bothered by the fat chick taking off?'

'What do you want, Marco?'

'No answer? Interesting. It's good to see you back in the game.'

'Marco …'

'I've got a journalist coming to talk to me about the contribution that the business makes to the Venetian community by hosting the Carnevale Masque, but I have an issue with the Swiss office that needs immediate attention. Can you handle the reporter? You know more about it all, anyway, since you're the boss.'

'I don't deal with media. That's your job.'

'I know that Raf and any other day, I'd do it. But I can't be in two places at once.'

Raf scoured a hand through his curls. 'When is he coming?'

'It's a she, and she should be here in fifteen minutes.'

'You don't give me much warning. Name?'

'Chelsea Willows.'

'And does she have anything to do with this?'

He held the paper out to his cousin. Splashed across the front page was an image of Raf and the beauty on Saturday night, both with masks in place. The headline destroyed his anonymity—*Ducolletti: Booty Call.*

'*Merda!* How would they know it was you unless they'd staked you out? And the morning after photo with Butterworth. Long-range, blurry. Do you think this mystery woman set it up?'

Raf ran a hand over his head again. 'I don't think so. If they knew who she was, they'd have used her name.'

'You're right. But I'd still check out the Australian. You'll handle the reporter?'

Raf grunted.

'Thanks, Raf. And be careful. You don't want to add anything to this fire.'

Marco dropped the paper on his cousin's desk and gave a half-wave as he left the office.

Five minutes later, Raf's secretary rang through to say that Miss Willows had arrived.

Raf got to his feet and rounded the table to greet the woman. She was medium height, wearing a bright yellow blazer over a cream blouse and skirt. She had a nicely rounded figure and bright auburn hair contorted into a chignon.

His body responded to her nearness. Which was unusual. Only his Saturday night beauty had managed to prompt that reaction from him in the last three years.

When the woman's eyes met his, she did a double-take and glanced down at the folder she carried.

'You are Marco Fabriolo?' She seemed nervous.

'I am Rafaele Ducolletti. That's Marco's photograph you have, but he's busy this morning, so I've agreed to answer your questions.'

'Oh. Uh … I'll wait till he's available. Thank you for your time.'

She pivoted towards the door and Raf caught sight of a double-diamond birthmark on the back of her neck.

'Chelsea? Your name is Chelsea? It is you, isn't it? Why did you leave?'

She swung towards him, her mouth firm.

'Maybe your fat little fuck buddy had other things to do.'

Raf was taken aback for an instant and then frowned, remembering Marco's crass comment. He stepped towards her, tugged the folder from her grip and dropped it on top of the newspaper.

'For the record, Chelsea, a "fuck buddy" is not how I thought of you. You blew my mind. I wanted to see you again.'

He held her eyes and drew her to him, wrapping his arms around her and dipping his mouth to hers. Her stiff body capitulated—she leaned into him.

He plucked open the buttons on her jacket and her blouse, and slipped his hand inside to cup her breast.

Her lips left trails of fire as they slid from his mouth to his open collar. She slipped the buttons loose on his shirt and smoothed both hands across his chest to spread the edges of the fabric apart.

He swivelled her around and sat her on the edge of his desk. His tongue plunged into her mouth.

'Wait here!'

He marched over and locked the door to his secretary's space.

In the ensuite on the other side of his office, he rummaged around in the drawers, desperate by the time he found one lonely condom secreted at the back. He hoped it didn't have a use-by date. It had been a while since he'd needed condoms.

He strode back to where Chelsea waited for him, still perched on his desk.

He slammed the foil package down beside her. 'If you don't want this to go any further, you should leave now.'

Chelsea held his gaze and slipped off the desk and onto her feet.

Disappointment burned like acid in his gut.

She stood before him, her expression unreadable. Then

she reached her hands behind her and her skirt slid to the floor, revealing a lacy skin-coloured thong that matched her bra. She stepped out of the skirt, bent down to retrieve it and placed it carefully on the visitor's chair beside him.

'You're staying.' His relief was palpable.

Her lips curved into a half-moon smile. 'I want another taste of you.'

He stepped in and cupped her buttocks, pulling her closer. One touch of her bare flesh and his cock was hard as a rock.

Her fingers worked at his belt and then the zipper of his trousers, and her hand slipped inside his briefs. She groaned deep in her throat—the sound had him poised to go off like a waterspout, but he wasn't a schoolboy anymore.

He pulled out her hand, grabbed the condom and his trousers, and led her over to sit on the large sofa at the ensuite end of the office. He eased her back and his thumbs smoothed the thong down her legs. He delighted at the feel of her thighs and calves as his fingers trailed along behind.

The thong dropped to the floor and he lifted her left leg onto his shoulder. He nudged her right one till her foot hit the carpet.

He closed his eyes and caressed the swell of her abdomen with his cheek.

She was beautiful, the scent of her intoxicating.

He inhaled deeply and moved lower. He used his nose to channel her intimate folds, allowing his mouth to reach its ultimate objective—the hard nub of her clitoris. He rested his top teeth there, running his tongue her from her perineum, along her slit and up to her clit.

She gave a muted squeak. 'Now, now, now! I need …'

Her urgency fuelled his. 'Um, ah. Where is …?'

He struggled to make sense of anything other than the rapture of being with her.

'I've got it.' He ripped the foil package open and rolled the rubber onto his cock. He tore off his trousers, socks and briefs and turned back to her.

'Please … ' she whimpered.

Who could resist a cry such as that? He grazed his teeth across the lace of her bra finding first one nipple and then the other.

She bucked again.

He pulled back and pushed himself into her. She was slick and ready. He withdrew again and plunged himself in to the hilt. Her muscles spasmed around him. She was close. Her hands tore at his hair. He thrust into her again and again. His mouth captured her scream as they both found their release.

He slumped onto her softness. '*Cara! Bella, bellissima.*'

He kissed the silky mounds that rose over the top of her bra cups and eased himself off her. He sat on the floor with his back resting against the sofa and felt her hand in his hair again, much more gently this time.

He reached out and grasped her ankle.

'Why would you not take off your mask for me?' He waited, one finger drawing circles around the bump on the inside of her ankle.

When she didn't respond, he looked up at her face. It was devoid of expression.

'You're wearing your mask again. Do I need to kiss it off?' His fingernails scraped up her calf.

The edges of her mouth turned up. 'You could try that, I suppose.'

Raf spun onto his knees and kissed her hard. 'Now, tell me why.'

'Because I'm not beautiful and I didn't want to scare you off.'

'Why would you think that? Who would tell you such nonsense?'

'My ex, er … just someone. And your friend agreed yesterday morning. I'm too round, not sexy enough, too bloody independent. I won't apologise for the last bit and I can't change the rest.'

Raf sprang to his feet and pulled her up to stand with him. The nakedness of their lower bodies met and sent a new fire fizzing through him.

'They're wrong.'

The phone on his desk rang. He strode across to bark at the intruder on the other end of the line.

'Your board meeting is due to start in fifteen minutes, sir.'

'*Merda.* Thank you, Sonia.' He turned back to Chelsea. 'I have a meeting soon. Can I see you tonight?'

'Give me your card and I'll let you know. There's a bathroom through there?'

She gathered up her clothes and sashayed into the ensuite.

Raf grabbed a wad of tissues from the box in the bottom drawer of his desk, dealt with the condom and dressed himself. He drew a tie and a jacket from the closet next to the sofa and was making final adjustments to his collar as Chelsea returned, looking immaculate. Even the chignon was back in place.

She couldn't hide the well-kissed lips, though. He smiled at that.

She returned his smile and strolled across to the desk to collect her folder. Raf could tell the moment she noticed the headline and the photograph of herself in the newspaper beneath the folder.

'This is me! What the hell!'

Raf narrowed his eyes. 'So, you had nothing to do with it? You didn't have a colleague doing a photo shoot of you enjoying life in Venice? Making you famous by capturing you with the city's reclusive bachelor?'

A new mask dropped over her features.

'Why would you even think that? Ah, because I'm a journalist and we're all devil spawn. If you thought that, what was this all about?' She waved a hand at the sofa. 'You think all this was some sort of set-up? That I would do that? Well, you're not the first I've had to deal with who had that opinion, and you're just as misguided.'

Moisture glistened in her eyes. She closed them and he watched her throat move as she swallowed.

'Shit!' She threw him a ferocious scowl. 'I didn't even know what the fuck you called yourself until I got here today, so how could it be a set-up? I came to meet with your PR guy, I might add, not you. Booty call, fuck buddy, accusations—I don't need this shit! *Arrive*-bloody-*derci*, arse-hole. I'll find my own way out.'

Raf reeled with the force of the passion that rolled off her as she stormed across the room and out the door, leaving it ajar behind her.

He couldn't be sorry that he'd prompted her outburst.

Passion. She had it in spades and he loved it.

***

CHELSEA'S ANGER kept her feet moving towards the office she was using while she was in Venice. It was the home of an Italian magazine from the same international stable as the one she worked for. She was nearly there when she veered into a café. Coffee or prosecco? Both reminded her of the bastard she'd just walked out on, but the prosecco might do more to calm her.

She finished her drink and stepped out into the *piazza*. The wind bit into her, reminding her that she still had the coat David Butterworth had lent her. Now would be the time to return it, while the shit-for-brains was in his meeting.

The navigation apps for Venice were notoriously unreliable, so she stopped at the office to pick up the bag that contained the coat and a map of Venice with the address she needed to find.

She made a few false turns along the way, but stood outside the front door of the address twenty minutes later. She banged the brass knocker.

David Butterworth opened the door as a scowling Rafaele passed through the foyer.

'Ah, Miss Chelsea. It's lovely to see you again.'

'You too, David.'

Rafaele stepped over to join them. Confusion flitted across his face. 'Chelsea. You came.'

'To see David.'

'Butterworth? You came to see Butterworth?'

She turned to the butler. 'Here's the coat you lent me. I've had it cleaned, so it's ready for the next damsel in distress. There's a little something in there for you, too. Thank you, again.'

'You're most welcome, Miss Chelsea.'

Chelsea turned on her heel to retrace her steps to the office.

'Damsel in distress? What? Chelsea!' Rafaele's voice boomed out.

Chelsea flicked her right hand into a stiff stop sign without turning and kept marching. She was back at her desk in ten minutes. It was amazing how temper could speed your steps.

She emailed Marco Fabriolo with the list of questions she had planned to ask him. She could receive the responses at home in Sydney and write the article there. She didn't need to be in Venice any longer.

Just as the office was closing for the long lunch break, a package arrived addressed to her. Inside was a magnificent white and red mask and a ticket to that evening's exclusive Carnevale Masque. The note read, 'Wear this for me, and I will find you. R.'

She looked again at the mask. It truly was beautiful. The white cap would cover the wearer's head and the thick red crescent, encrusted with sequins and diamantes, sat high and would cover the left half of the face.

But go to the masked ball? The company had tried to get tickets for her and Mel, her colleague and travelling companion, but there hadn't been any available. They'd sold out well in advance. And now she had one in her hot little hands.

Before she could change her mind, she passed the package and the ticket to Mel. 'The magazine needs this insider opportunity. You go. I'm going back to Sydney.'

* * *

Raf scanned every elaborate mask that entered the ballroom of the *palazzo*. When he finally spotted the bespoke red and white mask, it was not worn above the body he craved. He stormed over to the interloper.

'Where's Chelsea?'

'She's gone.'

'Gone where?'

'Home to Sydney. Her water taxi dropped me here before taking her to the airport.'

Raf felt as though his world had disappeared from beneath him.

He swallowed hard and turned to an usher who guarded an array of masks. 'I'll have that gold one, please.'

He swung back to Mel. 'This mask will go much better with your outfit. Would you mind returning the one you are wearing to me?'

Mel nodded and quickly complied.

'Your table number is on your ticket. When you get there, tell Signor Fabriolo that I had to leave, and he must make the speeches. Do you understand?'

As the woman nodded, Raf spun and sprinted to the dock where his boat and driver waited. 'The airport!'

At the airport jetty, Raf grabbed the sparkly red mask and flew up the stairs, dodging travellers and suitcases. He didn't care that he probably looked demented wearing a mask and a dinner suit amongst the casually attired throng.

He spotted Chelsea standing towards the rear of a long queue at a ticket desk.

'Chelsea!'

She couldn't have heard him over the noise of the airport, but she turned in his direction. Her face was free of makeup and she looked miserable. Still, to him, she was beautiful.

She stood immobile as he approached and didn't resist as he pulled her into his arms.

'Come, we can talk over here where it's less noisy.' He led her to an alcove a short distance away.

He looked into her tear-stained face and brushed his thumbs beneath her eyes. 'You didn't get to wear your mask.'

'It's a beautiful mask. Thank you for the thought, but it's time for me to go home. Goodbye … I still don't know what the hell to call you—Signor Ducolletti, treacherous bastard, what?'

Ah, there was some fire there still.

'Raf, just Raf. You can't leave yet. You must try on the mask.'

'Why?'

Raf grinned. 'If I slip your mask next to mine, what do you see?'

Her face transformed with a soft, sad smile. 'A heart! A magnificent, shiny heart.'

'Now can you see why no one but you could wear it? Only you can make my heart whole. I haven't trusted a woman with my heart since my fiancée fell for my cousin. Then I saw you in the square and I had no choice but to speak to you. You had my heart from that moment.'

'But you didn't trust me. You accused me of setting you up!'

'Stupid reflex. Today, in my office, I couldn't resist you, no matter what I thought you'd done. Stay with me.'

'You know nothing about me. I might be the sort of woman who would do things like that.'

'Then give me time to find out. Don't go. Let's see where this path will lead us.'

'And my job?'

'My hope, *cara*, is that you will find one here in Venice. My greater hope is that you will be too busy with me to want one.'

Raf took a breath and set the mask on her head.

'Stay with me. You came to Carnevale because we were meant to meet. Up until now, I've avoided being with a woman—trust issues,—but you found me anyway. Be my other half.'

'It might not work!'

'*The flight to Dubai is now boarding …*'

Chelsea turned her head as if in answer to the loud-speaker's call.

Raf tilted her chin towards him.

'Stay. Please! Give us a chance.'

She hesitated, just as she had on the night they'd met. This time, it was she who took his hand. An impish smile formed on her face.

'How can I resist?'

Raf's shout of 'Yes!' had people turning in their direction. He didn't care. He wrapped his love in a blinding, heartfelt kiss that he hoped would never end. Never.

Unmasked

FIONA M MARSDEN

'ARE YOU OKAY?'

The rasping words came out of the darkness, curling around her gut and settling in her chest.

Ree stood still, pressed back against the door, closing her eyes against the gloom. In the silence, she could almost hear something. A whisper of sound like the soft breathing of someone not quite relaxed. Slow and steady, but not naturally so. A little too deep, with a slight rasp at the turn of the exhale.

She mastered her own breathing. 'Yes. I'm fine.'

Her earlier reconnoitre had been well planned. Even with her eyes shut, she could make her way around the sparsely furnished room. She visualised it all in her mind. One king size bed to her right, nightstands on each side. Built-in wardrobes and the entrance to the en-suite bathroom to her left. A chair near the heavily draped windows in front of her. The décor was a sombre dark green with gold trim. The only thing she couldn't visualise was the man.

She kept her tone low and deep, and opened her lids. 'I'm letting my eyes adjust.'

Now there were small things her sight could pick up. The insignificant red glow of the fire alarm system on the ceiling. The brighter numbers on a clock beside the bed. A rim of pale light at her heels, coming underneath the door from the dimly lit hallway of the club. There was no corresponding rim where the bathroom door should be.

'Can you see?' He spoke again and she swivelled, squinting into the gloom.

'No. Can you?'

The rough exhale from the darkness signified relief. 'Only your silhouette as you came in.'

He was totally paranoid about being seen. Perhaps he had good cause. 'You're John?'

'And you're Ree, I presume.' There was a moment of hesitation. 'The surrogate.'

'Yes.' Not her full name, her proper name. That had no place here.

A gravelly chuckle warmed her nerves. 'Pleased to meet you, Ree.'

Something in the movement of the air warned her and she held up her hand.

A hand fumbled at her wrist. Fingers ran lightly over the back of her hand and then clasped it, sending tingles along the skin. She resisted the temptation to snatch her hand back and took a calming breath.

'And you, John.'

'John is not my real name.' He said it like he hated the subterfuge.

'Confidentiality is guaranteed. You could use your own name.'

The warmth of his touch withdrew. 'I don't think so.'

She shifted her feet as the silence lengthened. Then his voice came from further away. 'How do we do this?'

'This is your first experience with a surrogate?'

It was her first time as one, but he didn't need to know that.

'Yes.'

Even with the brevity of the word, she sensed the clenching of his jaw. It was part of her skill set, listening to people and hearing what they didn't say.

'It's about being comfortable and relaxed. It's not necessary for anything to happen this session.'

'It better.'

His words were a low mutter, but she heard them. Perhaps the darkness was responsible for her highly tuned senses.

There was something in the words, a raw anger that permeated the room. Not unusual for a man with his history.

A rustle of fabric gave her direction. She stepped slowly across to the sound, halting as her foot brushed against fabric. 'We'll begin then.'

'I'm ready.'

A warmth beside her had her shifting uneasily. She'd assumed he was on the bed, but from the texture of the silky fabric piled at her feet, he'd only been stripping back the heavy covers.

'John?'

A puff of air fanned her cheek. 'I'm here. What do you want me to do?'

'Are you undressed?'

'Yes.'

Something balled at the base of her throat. *Anticipation.* 'Is it all right for me to touch you?'

The warm air shifted again, cooling her forehead. She

wiped the nervous perspiration away with the sleeve of her robe, waiting for his consent.

'Go ahead.'

With slow movements, she reached out to where she guessed his chest level would be. It was satin and heat, searing her palms as she flattened them on his pecs. A sigh escaped unbidden, in tandem with a harsh indrawn huff from her client, his chest rising against her touch.

She smoothed her hands over the hard muscle, sweeping lightly across his nipples, stirring another sharp reaction. Moving up, her fingers encountered roughness— a combination of hard ridges and smooth, almost too smooth, skin. It lacked the warmth of the skin over his pecs.

His voice came again as she hesitated. 'Now you know why.'

Ree fought to keep her words steady. 'These are the burn scars?'

'Some of them. There are plenty more.'

'Are you comfortable with me touching them?'

There was a pause and another of those harsh inhalations. 'It's more about whether you can bear to touch them.'

'That's not an issue.'

It appeared to be working, keeping her voice at that low, nearly monotonous level. She couldn't let him catch any emotion. Anything he might question.

She continued her exploration, running her palms over his shoulders and down his arms. The scarring eased below the biceps but thickened again at the back of his forearms and hands. There were questions she needed to ask, even if she were aware of some of the answers.

'Fire?'

'A car accident. A fuel truck lost control on the freeway.'

She flinched at the horrendous image that flashed into her mind. 'Are there any other complications? Mobility issues I should be aware of.'

'Broken bones, but they've healed.'

'Psychological?'

'I don't remember the accident. Otherwise …'

Muscles rippled under her fingers as his shoulders raised slowly and dropped.

'Do you remember when it happened?'

The answer came slowly. 'Twelve … no … thirteen months ago.'

'And you've had problems with intimacy since your recovery.'

He stiffened under her touch and she let her hands drop.

His tone rasped. 'I don't want to talk.'

She could feel him distancing himself, physically as well as mentally. 'I need to have some indication of your physical and mental condition. I don't want to trigger any discomfort.'

The bedclothes rustled and shifted as he flopped onto the bed.

'Are you wanting to continue, J-John?'

Ree held her breath for his reply.

She heard nothing but the sound of movement on the bed, the crisp cotton sheets rubbing against each other and against the skin of the restless man. What would he look like against the white linen? This would be much easier with even a small amount of light, but the disadvantages were greater. This wouldn't be happening without the masking darkness.

'Yes. I want to continue. What do you need to know?'

Moving carefully, guiding herself with fingers lightly stroking the sheets, Ree sat on the edge of the bed. 'Whatever you want to tell me. Do you have a relationship?'

'Not anymore.'

It struck her deep in the chest, the wanton loneliness of that bleak statement. She knew how that felt.

'You broke up?'

'Yes … no. I don't know. But I wasn't taking this … body, this face, home to her. She deserves better than this horror.'

'But you are planning on having relationships in the future?'

The silence was telling.

'No.'

'Have you had any sexual relations since the accident?'

'No. I tried, but the woman freaked out. It wasn't working anyway.' A wry tone entered his voice. 'We men can't fake it when we aren't into it.'

'She was disturbed by your appearance?' A bubble of anger threatened to impinge on her voice and Ree swallowed it down.

'Couldn't bear to touch me, and when it came down to it, I didn't want to touch her. All very humiliating.'

'That's why you want to be in darkness?'

'Partly. I thought, if I couldn't see them—I mean, you —I could imagine. Isn't that what surrogates do? Take the place of someone else?'

'To some extent. Let me make sure I'm understanding this. You want to pretend I'm someone else, and you believe this will help you reach intimacy.'

'I suppose so. Is it a problem?'

He sounded sulky. Embarrassed?

'Not at all.' Her heart was pounding, and she pressed

her hand against her chest as if that would muffle the sound. She had to keep going. She had to ask.

'Is there a particular name you want to use?'

'Rosemary. Rose.'

Ree sucked in a deep breath. This was harder than she'd imagined, pretending to be someone else. She wasn't that person. Wasn't good at deception. But she could do it for him. She had made the choice to come here, knowing that it would be tough.

'All right. From now on, I'm Rosemary.'

'Rose. When we were … you know … I called her Rose.'

Breathe deep. 'Rose it is.'

'Can I touch you? What are the rules?'

'The rules are simple. If I say stop, you stop. If you are uncomfortable, you say stop and I stop.'

'I can do anything I want, if you agree?'

'Anything you would do with Rose.'

THIS WAS all kinds of fucked up. Jake knew he was fooling himself, but at least with this woman, it might be possible to get back something of his life. Not Rose. That ship had vanished with speed over the horizon.

She hadn't come near him after the accident. But later she'd had second thoughts. After that single disastrous visit, he'd been smart enough to tell the staff to refuse her admittance. Elegant, feminine Rose didn't need to face this horror in their bed. She would be kind, her lovely voice would soothe and cajole, but it would be pity. She was a damned psychologist. She would want to help. He'd put up with a lot of pain through his rehab, but her pity would be the worst kind of pain.

He sucked in air and tasted the unfamiliar musky scent of the surrogate. Different to the perfume Rose wore, which had a delicious herbal tang, but there was a hint of something underneath that triggered the same arousal. His ex was still there in his head. He had to get her out of it. With sex. He had to move forward.

'Ree? Can I touch you now?'

This, at least, was something. His hand had been doing double duty for months now. But even that only had the desired effect when it was Rose he was fantasising about. Rose with her gentle curves and long, well-toned legs. She always complained about being overweight, but he'd loved the softness. Loved the way she melded against him, pale silk against his darker gold.

'J-John?'

'Sorry. I guess I'm nervous.'

She sounded nervous too. Something about her voice.

They hadn't given him much information about the surrogate. His choice, he didn't want to know, but she must be young. Younger than his own thirty-four years.

He sensed movement and then a dip in the bed, along with a rustle of silk as if she were stripping off her robe.

His gut tightened at the recollection of the feel of her hand. Something visceral stirred low in his pelvis, giving him hope that the famine might be over at last.

For a moment, he half wished the light could be on. He wanted to see her, only that meant she would see him. Not something he would wish on anyone. Certainly not on a woman he hoped to have sex with tonight.

She shifted, and for the first time he caught the movement, a faint silhouette against the glow of the clock. Short hair. Wispy with a slight curl.

Memory swamped him, stealing air from his lungs. Rose, with her thick wavy hair right to her waist. The copper highlights in the chestnut catching the light. It was the one thing she let get out of control. This woman had a similar effect on him, physically. Enough to want to forge ahead.

'I'd like to start by touching you. Get an idea of your shape.'

Her voice came low and steady. 'How would you like this to happen?'

'If you lie down in the middle of the bed?' This whole thing was awkward, but for the first time since the accident, his body was eager.

She shifted, and he ran his hand lightly over her to get an idea of her position. 'Will it bother you if I sit astride your legs?'

'Go ahead.' Her low voice sounded stressed.

He settled down over her, taking the weight on his knees. The warm flesh pressing against his thighs triggered a reaction from his dick. The condoms were on the bedside table. He didn't need them yet, but with a surge of hope, he knew he'd be wanting them.

'Tell me if I'm too heavy.'

'It's fine.'

The breathy tone was a shade higher than her normal speech, reminding him of … *shit* … everything reminded him of Rose.

He stroked from her shoulder to her hips with both hands. Thinner than his former lover, but with a similar spread from narrow waist to curvy hips.

Her breathing was shallow, her body taut under his fingers.

'If you don't like what I'm doing, I'll stop.'

'No … it's … quite pleasant.'

Jake instinctively recognised the soft tremor of her body and her tightly controlled response. His nose caught the scent of arousal and his libido soared. *Fucking hell.* He was already sweating with the heat of it, matching the dew under his fingers. She wanted it, but she was holding back, trying not to respond overtly to his touch.

'It's okay. I want you to enjoy it. Need you to respond.'

Her body melted under his as she let go. It felt good. Hauntingly familiar.

His body vibrated with the need for action. He gripped the base of his shaft, tightening his hold until the urgency eased. Much as he wanted to get on with the fucking part, he knew he should hold off until he was certain she was comfortable with it. Even if it was her job.

The thought sat uncomfortably. He wasn't usually possessive. Except with Rose. But in all their time together, he'd never been jealous or uncertain of her commitment. He pushed the thoughts away as they had an inevitable effect on his erection. *Focus.*

He dipped his head to taste her skin, starting with the soft smoothness at the base of her throat.

Did all women taste the same? He couldn't remember. He'd hadn't been with another woman since he'd met Rose at his sister's eighteenth birthday party. The others all blended into a homogenous past. He barely remembered their names, never mind how they smelled or tasted. He'd been grateful for them, but they weren't Rose.

The woman his brother-in-law had matched him up with a couple of months ago hadn't got close enough for him to taste her. No spark, no chemistry at all. He and his dick had gone home more relieved than disappointed.

'Touch me.' He grated it out, hoping to drive away the past. The guilt he'd felt, still felt, at trying to put a woman in Rose's place. *She didn't want you.*

He leaned into her touch, loving the way she smoothed

her palms over his shoulders and came to rest on the rapid pulse on each side of his neck. Halting at the barrier.

'Are you wearing a mask? A balaclava?'

Something in her voice brought out a defensive streak. 'It's a compression bandage. It keeps the new skin grafts flat.'

'Do you need it all the time?'

It had been weeks since he'd been given the all clear to stop wearing it. 'Not really. I thought you'd prefer it to touching my scars.'

'I don't mind.' Her hand sought out his shoulder and rubbed over the surface with gentle yet firm strokes. 'It's only skin. Not like you have some horrible contagious disease.'

'No diseases.'

The darkness made a good mask. His eyes had adapted enough to detect movement, or even shape, but no detail. He was safe enough.

<hr>

REE LET out a sharp breath when the harsh rip of Velcro being undone broke the silence. He was still holding out on her. Wearing a mask, even under the shadow of darkness. But she wanted it all. Needed to know the truth, if only through touch.

He sat still, his thighs hard against her hips.

'Kiss me?' She sounded needy, but he complied, flattening his body against hers. The hard ridge of his erection pressed into the hollow beside her pelvic bone. She ached for it, ached for him.

The first brush of his mouth on hers was fire and ice, a shuddering contact that shot straight to her belaboured heart and heated her belly. It triggered a rapid pulse, beating hard and steady down low. An achy restlessness attacked her limbs and she squirmed to increase the contact, wrapping her arms around his neck and holding tight.

His tongue met hers with a wet slickness that echoed the dampness between her thighs, the cool drip of moisture from his erection. His hands explored her skin, pinching and squeezing her breasts, cupping them to rub the nipples against the firm velvet of his chest. He felt different, yet the same, all hard muscle underneath healthy skin and damaged tissue alike.

She gasped as he pulled away, releasing her legs from their confinement.

'Please …'

'Condom.'

She hadn't even thought of protection, knowing he'd been celibate.

'Good thought.' It came out breathless as she heard the crackle of foil. Any thoughts were swamped by sensation as he lifted her legs to wrap around him and brought his mouth back down.

'Ready, Rose?' He expelled the words against her lips.

She jerked under him at the intensity of his tone, and he smothered her mouth before she could query why. He probed the damp folds between her thighs and with the impact of tongue and fingers her brain fried.

Later. She'd think about it later.

He entered slow and deep, filling the emptiness, filling her. Her chest clamped over her wildly beating heart, a ball of emotion clogging her throat. The need was killing her. Sensation swirled and tightened and rippled as he struck a rhythm, his tongue and mouth blocking her voice, swallowing whimpers and words alike. He tasted of him, a hint of coffee and mint and happiness. Happiness. All gone, all lost.

Her body convulsed and the prickle in her eyes softened into tears.

He released her mouth to shout wordlessly into the darkness, shuddering into her as his rhythm broke into tremors that fed the last ebb of her orgasm.

'Oh God, Jake. Yes!'

He stilled mid-withdrawal and his hand came over her face, covering it. The scent of him and her combined overwhelmed her senses. With a movement that was close to a caress down her face, he withdrew, flopping onto the bed beside her.

She stayed silent, hoping he hadn't noticed her giveaway.

The mattress shifted as he moved away.

'Bitch.'

The overhead light came on at the flick of a switch, Jake standing tall and ominous by the bedside table. Her lungs stalled at the first sight of him in over a year. The scarring wasn't a surprise. She'd run her hands over most of the damage in the dark. He still looked amazing, his tall frame well-muscled.

'Did you think I wouldn't recognise you when I was inside you? For fuck's sake, Rose. How thick do you think I am?'

Rose averted her stare from his manhood, resisting the obvious retort. 'We haven't seen each other for over a year. We've both changed. I didn't know what would happen.'

'Why would you do something like this? What kind of kick did you get from violating my trust?'

'I … nothing. I wanted to help. Wanted to see you.'

'See me?' The rough gravel in his voice grated on her ears. 'Is this what you came to see?'

He stood directly under the harsh overhead light. It showed every crease and blotch of colour on his ravaged face. The damage to his right ear, missing a lobe, and the glossy tight skin on his scalp above the ear where no hair grew. He'd shaved the rest to match. It was ugly, but not as bad as she'd imagined.

She shrugged, suddenly conscious of her nakedness under his dismissive gaze. 'So, you have a Deadpool thing happening. Some people might count that as a plus.'

He came closer, leaving the circle of light behind. The shadows painted the damage in ridges and hollows. There'd been extensive work done; she could tell by the different skin tones. His right eyelid drooped like melted wax, but the eye was bright and accusing.

'Why did you have to come?' The rasp scratched at her ears.

'I wanted to help.'

'I don't. Need. Your pity.'

A curl of anger stiffened her spine. 'I don't give pity fucks.'

'What do you call what we did then?'

'Making love?' Her voice squeaked at the higher register and she pressed her hand to her throat.

His eyes dropped to the action of her hand as it pushed the woven leather band against her skin. Something stirred in the depths, a softness in his gaze pushing out the anger.

'What happened to your voice?'

'Nothing. I strained it.'

His long fingers, blotchy and scarred, reached up to brush against her hand. He frowned, rubbing the tips of his fingers together.

'Show me.'

Only the truth mattered now. She fumbled with the

buckle and drew the collar away, letting her hand hang limply at her side.

Head tilted, Jake studied her throat. He traced the longer scar with one finger and lingered at the thicker patch in the centre.

'When did it happen?' His tone had gentled, as if he already knew.

'In the accident.'

'You got out before the explosion?'

'My side of the car wasn't as damaged. The door opened easily.'

'But you injured your throat.'

'The seatbelt. It saved me going through the windscreen. Swings and roundabouts.' She tried smiling, but he only stared at her.

'Is that why you couldn't come to visit me at first.'

'I was on a ventilator for several days. My vocal cords were paralysed.'

The undamaged brow rose. 'You couldn't talk? When you came to visit later.'

She shook her head.

'Shit.' He turned away, rubbing his hand over the smooth surface of his head. 'I thought it was me. I thought looking at me stunned you speechless.'

'I was shocked. You were like a mummy, all wrapped up from head to toe. All I could see, anyway.'

He spun to face her. 'At least I could talk.'

Between them lay the cruelty of the words he'd spoken, sending her away. The hospital staff had been instructed to keep her out.

'It didn't matter. You were in pain.'

'It mattered. I wanted you with me. Needed you.' His brow furrowed in a curiously uneven way, the damaged side remaining smooth. 'Did you ever come back? Try again?'

'A few times.'

'They didn't tell me.'

'I asked them not to. I thought it might upset you. The doctor said peace of mind was essential to the healing process.'

He laughed and it cut off short. 'The doctor? If only he'd known the truth. I ached for you, Rose. Every. Fucking. Day.'

'Me too.' She'd have broken a drought with her tears in those first months until she'd formulated a plan. And then this opportunity had come up.

His head cocked to one side, half-turning as if to hide the worst of the damage. 'What have you been doing?'

The tension between them eased at his change of subject.

She reached for the robe beside the bed, aware of his gaze following her. When she'd finished tying the belt and made herself comfortable, he moved, picking up a pair of black boxers from the floor. Instead of joining her on the bed, he sat on the dark green bucket chair by the window. He wasn't that far from her, but it seemed greater. He sat, half-turned away, his injuries shadowed from the glare of the overhead light.

On impulse, she turned the bedside lamp on and flicked the ceiling light off. Immediately, she could see Jake relaxing, leaning back in the chair, turning his face directly to her.

'Better?'

He nodded. The light barely reached him, showing a softened, not quite blurred version of his face. She could almost imagine him as he'd been, despite the loss of that thick head of blond hair.

It was vital to be open and honest. 'I've done very little. I couldn't work because of my voice. I'm not supposed to overstrain it, and lecturing and private patients are all about talking.'

'Will you be able to go back to it later?'

'I've been doing research projects. Mostly as an assistant, but I've got some ideas.'

'You aren't doing the surrogate thing as a regular gig?'

Her skin heated. 'No. I don't have the right psychological makeup for the job.'

'Neither have I.'

Her foot jerked, hitting the bedside table with a thump.

That raspy chuckle warmed the gap in her heart.

'No, sweet Rose, I'm not planning to use my rediscovered prowess in people's bedrooms. Other people's bedrooms.' His hands smoothed down over his knees and rested there. 'I've been discharged from the navy.'

JAKE WATCHED FOR A RESPONSE, knowing how much she'd hated the long absences, the demanding schedule of his life as a navy pilot. Instead of the smile he expected, she frowned.

'I'm sorry, Jake. You must be devastated.'

'I thought you'd be pleased.'

'You loved what you did. Won't you miss it?'

'I have partial hearing loss in my right ear.' He automatically touched it and flinched at the hard ridge that bordered where his lobe used to be. 'I can still be rated to fly as a civilian, but not in the defence forces.'

'What will you do?'

He hesitated, studying her face, her body language. 'You aren't repulsed by what you see?'

'I have to be honest, it's not attractive. You aren't the pretty boy I met nearly ten years ago. But I'm not exactly model material either. Change is inevitable.'

Her hand went up to her throat and he saw again the barely visible discolouration to the skin on her hands.

'Did you get burned as well? I thought you got out all right.'

Her colour surged, pinking the pale skin of her throat and darkening her cheeks. 'I went back for something.'

'Why would you do something so stupid?'

She remained silent, rubbing the tips of her fingers over the back of her hands.

Nausea wrenched at his gut. 'You went back for me.'

He flung himself across the floor to kneel at her feet. Taking her hands, he looked at the blotchy skin in the light of the lamp. 'Did you drag me out?'

'Only part of the way. I couldn't lift you.'

She wasn't small, but he was a big guy and would have been a dead weight. 'What happened when the car exploded?'

'Someone dragged me away, but it exploded before they could go back for you. It threw you into the air.'

'That's how I got the broken bones?'

Her hands twitched under his. 'Most of your burns were from the initial fire.'

'Did you see?'

'Yes.' It came out as a whisper.

'How could you bear it? How can you look at me now without disgust?'

'You're still Jake. Still you. For better or worse.'

He fingered the bare knuckles on her left hand. Before the accident, she'd worn his ring. They'd been coming driving to Brisbane for the wedding because both their families lived here. The accident had occurred on the freeway only an hour from their destination.

'What did you do with your ring?'

'I have it at home.'

'Home?'

'My unit here. The lease came up for renewal earlier in the year. I moved back in after I packed up the place at Jervis Bay.'

Jake nodded. 'I've been living with my parents.'

'I know. They still talk to me.'

'Is that how you knew?'

'That you were looking for sex? Your sister told me and put me in contact with the therapist.'

Jake buried his face in her stomach, the silky fabric of her robe cool against his cheek. 'I'm glad you came.'

'You aren't still angry?'

Her hand stroked over his scalp, not hesitating as it moved from shaven skin to scar tissue.

'No. I'm not angry.' He lifted his head to face her. 'At least it solved one of my problems.'

Her mouth twitched. 'Are you sure? I mean, anonymous sex might be your thing.'

'No.' He met her gaze, seeing the sparkle of tears that spoke more of her feelings than the light words. 'No. It was you. All you. It felt like you right from the start.'

The press of her lips on his forehead where smooth skin met with rough shivered through him.

'I want more, Jake. Need more. Please don't send me away again.'

'Never. We've had worse. It can only get better. If it's what you want?

She framed his face with her hands, no masks, no darkness between them. 'I want you. Always you.'

'You have me.'

Her mouth was soft under his and he wondered how he could have ever believed her to be someone else, even for a moment. Her taste, her scent, the gasping sighs. All were familiar. All were his Rose, his love.

'Will we try again, this time with the lights on? I want to see you.'

Her pink colour blossomed again, but she slid off her robe before he could strip his boxers. This time it would be for both of them. A renewal. Honest and real.

Unmasked.

The
Deepest Cut

DM INGLIS

'SCALPEL.'

'Scalpel!'

Jack felt the cold steel of the scalpel handle slap into his open palm. Hard. He turned his head slightly only to stare straight into a pair of emerald green eyes.

No!

Surely it couldn't be?

Not after all this time.

The eyes were the only part of her face visible. A cap covered her hair and a surgical mask extended from beneath her chin to the bridge of her nose. Goggles protected her eyes and a perspex shield extended the full length of her face, obscuring her it even more.

The eyes stared unblinkingly back. Not a skerrick of recognition in them. He shook his head and turned away. He still saw her everywhere. And it was like a punch to his gut.

'Where's Maria?'

The figure shrugged.

'I'm not sure. I've been allocated to your list today. Perhaps she's sick?' Her voice was low and husky.

'I need Maria. She knows what I like and when I need it.' Jack scowled.

'Well, today you've got *me*.' Her tone was clipped. 'To give you what you *need* and what you *like, doctor*.'

This woman sure had some attitude. And eyes that provoked memories he didn't want to deal with.

'Well, maybe. Just pay attention and try to keep up.' He turned back to the patient on the operating table. Abdomen exposed, yellow-brown smears of the betadine preparation wash giving the skin a jaundiced appearance.

'I'll need you here. Next to me.' He jerked his head, his hands poised, the circular lights above reflecting off the scalpel he still held aloft.

Jack sensed her move closer. He stiffened as a musky vanilla scent pervaded his nostrils. She even smelled the same for crying out loud.

Where the hell was Maria? No distractions there, just efficiency and unfailingly good humour.

'Can I get you something else, doctor?'

Her voice, low and melodic, shook him from his reverie. He looked around at the expectant faces of the surgical team.

'Someone turn on the music!' Jack snapped.

The theatre runner leapt to attention and Lady Gaga filled the room.

Right, concentrate man. He caught the eye of the anaesthetist, Rob. They always worked the same lists and were generally in sync. Now, Rob looked at him with eyebrows raised in silent question.

'All good at your end?'

Rob nodded. 'Yep, out cold. Obs are all good. Over to you now. Okay?'

Was Rob questioning whether he was okay to perform the surgery? Good Lord! Why wouldn't he be?

'Right.' He stood straighter. 'Incision at 0907. Let's go, team.' His scalpel contacted the skin and a perfect line appeared in its wake. He mopped at the blood as he incised through the skin layers, then the muscle and finally the peritoneum.

'Retractor,' Jack barked.

Hard steel slapped into his palm. His skin burned beneath the double layer of latex gloves that covered them. He spun his head, ready to admonish, and met the cool expression of *those* green eyes.

He narrowed his eyes and bit his tongue to stop the retort that wanted to erupt and would be sure to see him summoned to the human resources department. He'd better be careful about how he asked for the sharp objects. He was liable to lose a finger at this rate.

He turned back to the task at hand.

Abdominal cavity exposed, he probed with a finger, spreading the loops of small intestine, feeling along as he went until he located the spot he was after.

'Have a feel of this.' Jack held the loop between two fingers, the cancerous growth obvious beneath the membrane.

Green Eyes quirked an eyebrow at him.

'Yes, I'm talking to you. Have a feel of this. You're here to learn, aren't you?'

She slipped her hand down until it was adjacent to his. Her fingers slid along the shiny surface of the bowel. If her hands weren't inside someone's gut, he would have called the action sensual. He imagined those hands, *her hands,* caressing him as they once had.

Bloody hell. What was *with* him today? It was those darned green eyes. Gritting his teeth, he moved his body a couple of inches to the right, widening the gap between them.

'I can feel it.' Her voice was animated as her fingers continued to gently palpate the mass.

That voice. It had been months since he'd heard *her* voice everywhere he went. He still felt the ache of loss deep in his heart. She was gone. Out of his life forever and he had to bloody well get used to it.

'Ready with the sponges?'

'Ready.' She indicated the tray of implements. Neat rows of gauze clamped between the ridged end of long-handled forceps sat waiting. She was organised. Good. He hated working with anyone new. He liked things done a certain way.

Jack incised the bowel and quickly identified the tumour boundaries. It was encapsulated. Excellent news.

'Sponge.' He held his hand out without moving his eyes.

Slap. He flinched as the metal handle whacked into his hand.

'Not so *bloody* rough with the instruments.' He growled, resisting the temptation to open and close his hand to minimise the residual ache.

'So *sorry*, doctor. I thought *you* weren't using social conventions … today.'

He looked around. Her eyebrows were raised and her eyes opened a little wider than before. Long lashes with a lick of black mascara, a contrast to the green. The same tiny flecks of brown dotted the iris.

She looked pissed off. And it completely threw him.

'Sorry?' Jack was confused.

'That's much better.' She dipped her head slightly. 'Shall we continue?'

Who the hell did she think she was? He was the

surgeon here and this was his operating theatre! He ground his teeth.

'You might want to clamp that bleeder, doctor.'

Jack forced his focus down. *Concentrate, man!*

He inserted the gauze pad and mopped at blood oozing from the incision site until he could visualise the source.

'Clamp.'

Thwack.

Fuck. He could feel the heat rush to his face and knew his skin would be a fierce red. But not as red as the pool that had appeared in the cavity. His hands rushed to clamp the errant vessel.

'Diathermy'—he gritted his teeth and hissed—'*please.*' He felt the diathermy wand press gently into his hand.

The rest of the operation went without a hitch. He was washing up when Rob appeared beside him.

'All good in recovery?' Jack asked.

'Yep, no problem. He's waking up nicely and vitals are all good.' Rob soaped up his arms before rinsing the froth into the sink below. 'So, no Maria today?'

'No.'

'Who's the scrub nurse that managed to throw you off your game, then?'

'It was that obvious?'

'Only to me. I've worked with you for a long time, Jack.'

'She reminded me of someone I used to know. That's all. Took me by surprise.'

Jack grabbed the end of the paper towel and jerked. He cursed when the roll unravelled, splaying loops into the wet sink, and quickly soaked up the water pooled at the bottom.

'Crap.' He scrunched the sodden mass into a ball and tossed it into the bin.

'Coffee before the next case?' Rob asked him quietly. 'Get your rhythm back?'

Jack nodded. He needed a distraction so he'd be able to focus on the next patient. Not on the green eyes etched in his mind.

The tearoom was full of operating theatre staff, all dressed similarly in scrubs of varying colours. No one colour differentiated roles and functions. Staff just grabbed a set off the dry-cleaning trolley at the start of each shift.

Jack looked around the room. The sterile theatre garb wasn't required in the tearoom. Only the scrubs worn beneath. Everyone looked completely different in here.

Was she a blonde? A brunette? Hell, the gowns were so shapeless he hadn't been able to tell if she was curvy or petite. All he knew was that her eyes were the same green. He knew it couldn't be her, but he had to see her without the mask and cap. To be sure.

***

ANNABELLE WATCHED as Jack entered the room two steps behind Rob the anaesthetist. He looked around as he walked in and Anna quickly cast her eyes downwards as his gaze swept her way.

Was he looking for *her*?

Why the hell would he be? He'd looked at her with annoyance, not recognition.

The minute she'd turned from arranging instruments on her tray, ready to start the procedure, she'd recognised him.

Fuck. She couldn't believe he worked here. It was the opposite side of town to where he lived.

And she knew *exactly* where he lived. She would *never* have taken this new position had she known.

His surgical garb couldn't hide that he was well put together. Broad shoulders that tapered to a V at his hips. Black hair, tousled from where he'd pulled off his surgical cap, curling along the collar of his shirt.

Pity he was such a jerk.

She was certain he hadn't recognised her, but that only made her feel more pissed off. One amazing night together. She'd thought it may have been the start of something new and exciting, but it had ended so very badly. For her. Clearly it had *no* impact on him. Her hands curled into fists in her lap.

Anna glanced up. He had his back to her as he made his coffee. She needed to speak to the unit manager and see if she could swap to another surgeon's list for the afternoon session. She wanted … no, needed to keep as much distance as she could between her and Jack Wellington.

She edged out through the nearest door.

Not possible, I'm afraid … short-staffed as it is … Is there a problem, nurse?

No, no. Of course there's no problem. Anna had been quick to reassure her manager who looked expectantly at her, waiting for her to expand on her reasons for the request.

Only that I was once head over heels in love with the surgeon.

Anna was hardly going to say that! Or that he'd swept her off her feet with passion and promises. And then had had devastatingly broken her heart.

And that he still had the same exhilarating effect on her.

'WELL, if we have to work together all afternoon, we should at least introduce ourselves. I'm Jack Wellington.'

Crap. As soon as she said her name, the game would be up. He'd surely remember her name … he had sent her roses every day for a week until she'd agreed to go out with him.

More fool her.

'I'm … Bella.' A derivation of her name that would evoke no memory for him. Hopefully.

'Bella, good. We've only got one case this afternoon. A big one, though, so we all need to be on our toes.'

His eyes crinkled and she imagined the smile beneath the mask. And the perfect white teeth and dimple in his chin.

A hand gently closed around her heart and squeezed. A lump formed in her throat and she swallowed around it. She nodded, not trusting her voice. Not because he might recognise it. That clearly hadn't happened. The eyes looking at her now were those of a polite stranger.

STANDING beside him as his long fingers worked skilfully was torture. She knew firsthand what magic those fingers could wield. Stand beside him, she had no choice but to do.

They worked in close confines over the exposed abdomen. His hip brushed against hers occasionally. Each a gentle, chance caress through the fabric of her scrubs and theatre gown.

A barrage of images invaded her mind. Jack gently cupping her face, stroking her cheek and hair. Lowering his beautiful, sensuous mouth to capture hers. Teasing before deepening the kiss, so every nerve in her body sprang to life. This man had wooed her and courted her until she'd been putty in his hands. And she had returned every kiss and every touch with equal hunger.

Stop it now! She took a deep breath and forced the images from her mind.

'Everything okay, Bella?' Jack looked concerned. 'Not feeling too hot or dizzy? Yell out if you need a break.'

Anna managed a weak nod. She had no doubt that her brow glistened with sweat. Just not for the reasons he thought.

'I'm fine. Thank you.' *Concentrate girl, for fuck's sake.*

SHE WAS GONE by the time he'd washed up and changed his clothes. Damn it. He needed to talk to her. One glimpse of her face. That's all he needed to reassure himself it wasn't her.

Or did he hope like hell it was?

He shook his head, beckoning for common sense to return. What if it *was* her? She'd made it clear she was only after a short, sharp fling.

Nothing more.

Besides, why else would she have carefully hooked him, played out the line, drawn it in to finally land him in her net only to toss him back?

After she'd taken what she wanted from him.

Not that it had taken much to land him in the end. He'd happily leapt right into the net.

From first sight, she'd been breathtaking. Green eyes with little brown specks that he had lost himself in. Brown hair, thick and wild, that his fingers had curled in as he pulled her face towards his. Lips as red and perfect as a new rose bud that had willingly opened beneath his. A tongue, sharp in wit and delightful in physical torture. A tongue that had made his lust skyrocket.

He'd been finishing his surgical program. Completing his final placement before he sat his last exams. He'd known time was running out to woo her before he moved on to his new role.

The planets had aligned perfectly. His kitchen renovations were about to be completed in time for him to start his new job as surgeon at Valley General. It had meant he'd be able to move out of his brother's house before his brother was due to return home to Australia.

And this brown-haired angel had agreed to have dinner with him. Though he'd hoped for a whole lot more.

———

ANNA SLIPPED out of the operating theatre and into the female change rooms while Jack was writing post-op instructions in the patient's chart. She wasn't ready for him to see her yet. She needed time to perfect her composure. To mask the hurt and pain that still burned her soul. To survive the indifference in his eyes.

Besides, she didn't trust herself not to give him a roundhouse punch, right in his perfect jaw.

The fury she still felt competed with her body's complete failure to obey her brain. And loathe him she should after what he'd done.

She had resisted him for several weeks, determined to stand by her philosophy to never mix work and pleasure. But oh no … he had sought her out, flirted, teased, flattered and finally broken down her guard.

What harm could dinner do after all?

But it had been dinner sans dessert in the end …

• • •

HIS KNEE PRESSED against hers beneath the table, his hand stroking in tiny circular motions as it moved higher. Sliding beneath her skirt and along the skin of her thigh. Caressing the silk fabric of her knickers. Overwhelming her senses until she couldn't focus on anything except what his hands were doing.

'Let's get out of here,' he murmured in her ear. She was already pushing back her chair.

She waited out the front while he settled the bill, grateful for the breeze cooling her flushed face. Turning as the door swung closed, she stepped towards him and into his open arms. He backed her into the shadows and his lips sought hers. Hungry, demanding, delicious.

'My place?' he murmured in her ear, his hands holding her buttocks against him. There was no doubting he was as turned on as she. She could feel his arousal pressing into her hip.

'Please,' she moaned breathily.

He drove, one hand on the steering wheel, the other twirled in her hair, caressing her cheek, her neck, her lips. Her hand, with a mind of its own, caressed his thigh, and she marvelled at the tautness, moving higher until her finger traced the outline of his erection.

He drew in a sharp breath, his knuckles white as he gripped the wheel.

The trip was short. Thank goodness. Jack pulled into the driveway and as soon as he silenced the engine, he unclipped his seatbelt and turned towards her. Cupping her face in his hands, their mouths met with equal lust.

They made it as far as the kitchen where he pulled her to him again. Devouring her mouth with his as his hands wreaked havoc on her carefully put-together outfit. He unzipped her skirt and she obligingly sashayed her hips to facilitate its slide to the floor, landing in a puddle of green silk about her ankles.

Jack's hands lingered momentarily as he caressed the lace of her knickers, gently teasing, sending electric impulses to her core. His hands slid upwards, taking her blouse with them. She lifted her arms to help.

'God, you're beautiful.' His words were husky.

She stood before him in her lingerie.

He stroked her breasts beneath the fabric and, as her nipples peaked, he rolled them gently between his thumb and forefinger.

Unable to contain her moan, she sagged against the kitchen bench, her knees weak. His hands deftly unclipped her bra and it joined the skirt on the floor. He lowered his mouth and teased her nipple with his tongue.

'Oh, Jack,' she whimpered, fumbling with his belt. Willingly, he assisted her to release it, kicking off his shoes and moving his hips to help her divest him of his pants. His erection strained against his underwear. Anna slid her hands inside, feeling his throbbing length before pushing his jocks down his thighs to the floor.

He half walked her, half carried her backwards until they reached the table. He lifted her and carefully lay her down so her buttocks were at the edge and her legs hung towards the floor. He hooked his thumbs beneath the elastic of her knickers, drawing them slowly along her thighs towards her feet.

They were both completely naked.

His knee between her legs widened the gap between her thighs. His hand filled it, parting her folds as he slid a finger inside. She almost lost it she was so incredibly aroused.

He leaned over, capturing her mouth with his. She returned the kiss with equal passion. His finger was joined by another and she could feel the tightness and wetness of her pussy. His thumb located her bud and caressed in circular motions as his fingers continued to stroke the sensitive inner wall.

Paroxysms of pure delight engulfed her completely, her body throbbing with the most exquisite sensations she'd ever encountered.

Jack held her as she cried out. As the waves subsided, he cupped her head and gently kissed her eyes, her nose and her mouth.

He slid her buttocks to the edge of the table and she could feel the tip of his erection probe her opening. She hooked her feet behind his back and drew him close.

She gasped as his length filled her. He pressed in until they were joined as one, pelvis against pelvis. He moved slowly at first, drawing out before thrusting back in. His eyes fixed on hers, his fingers teasing her nipples.

'You like?' he whispered huskily.

Anna could only nod. He increased the speed and pressure of his thrusts. She matched him, raising her pelvis up and pulling his buttocks closer with her legs wrapped about his hips.

He held her gaze as she drew close to release again. Having him watch her at her most exposed and vulnerable enhanced her arousal. She arched her back as the throbbing waves commanded her body.

'Anna.' He let out a strangled moan as he held her hips, thrusting deep inside until she felt the rhythmic contractions as he too found his release. They stayed like that, eyes locked, before Jack gathered her into his arms, holding her closely against his chest, his cheek against her hair.

Anna knew in her heart that she had found the man she wanted to spend the rest of her life with.

JACK DROVE home from the hospital. His logical mind told him the girl with the green eyes couldn't be Anna. There were similarities, sure. The green eyes for one. But a lot of people had green eyes with brown speckles.

The feeling of desolation he'd fought for months was back. Lodged in the pit of his stomach like a leaden weight. The new girl a reminder of dreams shattered and love lost.

He'd had the most amazing night with the woman he knew to his very core was destined to be his soul mate. They had held each other all night, had talked of hopes and dreams and wondered at the amazement they found in each other.

He'd woken and rolled over to pull her close. The sheets beside him had been cold. Frantic, he'd leapt from the bed and rushed to the kitchen. Her clothes had no longer been crumpled on the floor.

She had left.

His world had gone from exhilarating to crashing devastatingly to earth. For weeks, he'd called her phone, and each time it went to voicemail, he'd left a message begging her to return his calls.

Nothing. No response.

Eventually, he accepted that she'd ghosted him. In the most heartless, callous and cruel way.

He had moved home once the renovations were completed, started his new job and life had continued.

Time heals all wounds. He knew it to be true, he just wished it would hurry up.

Moments like this, when the bandaid was ripped from his healing wound, reminded him of how raw he still felt inside.

Damn Anna. For playing with him and then dumping him like a hot potato.

ANNA TOSSED and turned all night long. Should she return to work or quit and move somewhere far away from him? Well, she'd *done* that and look where that had got her. In the same hospital. In his operating theatre. What were the chances of that!

Her image in the bathroom mirror reflected the shattered woman who'd spent so much time and effort trying to heal after leaving Jack's place that ill-fated morning.

The anguish was the same now as she recalled the perfect night. And the heartbreaking morning afterward.

SHE LAY AWAKE, watching Jack sleep. So peaceful and content. Reaching out, she gently smoothed his hair from his face.

They had talked for hours and he'd told her he felt like he'd been hit by a steamroller, so powerful was her effect on him. She had listened to him speak, an idiotic grin on her face. She felt the same, she'd told him. They had lain close, talking about the future. Their future.

They'd made love again. Gently this time, without the urgency and now, sated, they lay together, her head on his chest. His heart thudding below her cheek, rhythmically comforting. She'd found her *person*, her *place*.

It was love she felt. She was certain. And he felt it too!

And it was going to be amazing.

She eased herself from beneath his arm to go to the bathroom. Why she opened the cabinet above the sink, she couldn't say. The familiar packet on the shelf caught her eye and she picked it up and read the label affixed.

'Mrs Isabel Wellington.'

Anna shoved it back in and closed the door. She leant forward with her hands on the basin and took a series of deep breaths.

There had to be a good reason why Jack would have someone's contraceptive pill in his bathroom cabinet. Someone called Isabel. He hadn't mentioned that he'd been married, but hell, plenty of people had a divorce under their belt.

Holding her breath, she pulled open another cupboard. A hair straightener sat on the shelf. The cord was carefully wrapped around the body so it stored neatly. It was a Cloud Nine—expensive and not something an ex-wife would likely leave behind.

Heart pounding in her ears, Anna reached for the pack of contraceptive pills. The date the prescription had been filled was two weeks ago. There were gaps in the row where some of the pills were missing.

The bastard.

She had to get out of there. What a complete fool she'd been! His wife goes out of town and he picks up a willing nurse from work to fuck for the night?

Once she was in the taxi, the tears flowed.

NOW, her image stared back. Run away again?

Hmm … maybe not. She was calmer now. In control. Able to conceal the hurt and wanting to show she *had* survived, that he was *nothing* to her. She'd proved that yesterday, as hard as it was to project cool indifference. But she'd done it.

He was the one who should feel awkward and embarrassed. Not her.

She pulled on her uniform and drove to work.

———

MARIA WAS BACK, beaming at him with her usual grin.

'I'm back!' she bellowed as she came into the scrub room where he was lathering his arms.

Jack returned her grin, but inside his heart sank. He realised he'd been looking forward to seeing Bella today. He liked her spirit. He liked her eyes. He needed to know that she was nothing like Annabelle.

He needed to move on.

———

THE ORTHOPAEDIC THEATRE couldn't have been more different. The noise levels for starters. It sounded more like a construction site than an operating theatre. And the surgeon was older and not one for chatter.

Anna looked for Jack in the tearoom throughout the day, but he mustn't have been operating today. Probably for the best. She'd worked herself up to anger and she didn't want to let rip at him at work. A day's grace to calm down would be good.

———

ANNA WALKED through the revolving hospital exit and headed towards the car park. No Jack. She'd been on edge all day, looking for him around every corner. Rehearsing what she would say. Fighting the anticipation at the prospect of a glimpse.

'Annabelle?'

Anna stopped.

His voice. No doubting it.

She clutched her bag closer to her side and slowly turned. Jack stood on the footpath opposite. He was panting as though he'd been running. His hands hung by his sides.

'It is you.'

Anna couldn't speak. Her rehearsed speech abandoned her.

Jack crossed the road and Anna swung away, walking briskly towards the car park.

His fingers closed around her upper arm jerking her to a stop.

'Oh no you don't. Not this time.' He swung her around to face him, his mouth set in a tight, scowling line.

'Let me go.'

His grip tightened as she tried to pull away.

'Not until you tell me why you ran away. It was a low act, Annabelle. Ghosting me like that.' He shook her arm. 'After *all* we talked about. After *everything* you said to me!' His face was red, his voice hard and cold.

What a goddamned cheek! Anna wrenched her arm free and rounded on him. She clutched her bag more tightly to her chest, though her instinct was to swing it and whack him hard with it.

'How dare I? How *dare I*?' She hissed the words around the knot of rage in her throat. 'Why don't you fuck off home to your *wife*, Jack?'

'My what?'

'Your *fucking* wife.' Tears sprang to her eyes and she angrily swiped them away.

'I don't have a wife.'

'Don't lie to me, Jack. I *saw* her contraceptive pill in the bathroom. Her *things* in the cupboards. *Isabel.*' Her tears fell unchecked as she swung around and strode off.

'*Isabel* is my sister-in-law!'

Anna stopped short and turned slowly back.

'What?'

'That was my brother's house. I was staying there while my kitchen was being renovated.' He walked toward her, stopping just out of arm's reach. 'That's why you ran away? You thought I was *married?*'

Anna nodded.

'You asked me if I wanted to go back to your place. I thought it was *your* place.'

'No … no. You crazy girl.' Jack closed the distance between them, hesitated momentarily, and then pulled her into his arms. She offered no resistance.

'Really?'

'I meant every word I said to you that night. I was … am in love with you, Annabelle. Anna. *Bella.*'

Anna could feel his heart pounding beneath her cheek as his arms pulled her tighter.

'Please, tell me you meant it too?' he murmured against her hair.

'Oh my god.' Anna's mind was in a whirl. What was he saying to her? Was it true? She looked up at him and saw his earnest expression and his anxious frown.

'Please, Anna, tell me you meant it too.'

'Jack, I meant every word. I was so *devastated* that I had to go. You broke my heart that night.'

'Can we go somewhere and talk? Please?'

Anna nodded.

'We can pick your car up later. I'm not letting you out of my sight until we sort this out.' He grinned wickedly at her. 'Besides, I want to show you my new kitchen!'

Her Outback Seduction

CL ROSE

AS YET ANOTHER dust storm blasted the small town of Wingillie, Bonnie Wright finished reading her latest regency romance novel and put it down with a dreamy sigh. The old post office come general store was not dust-proof. Bonnie noted the motes drifting on the shaft of sunlight glaring down from the central skylight. A fridge whirred away in the background, every now and then giving a flurry of pops.

With another sigh Bonnie looked across the road towards the old weatherboard pub partially hidden behind the veil of dust that swept down the main street. Tonight, was pot-and-parmie-night. Pity it wasn't hot-single-man-night, although if it were, they'd have to ship in a truckload of hotties from Brisbane. Her libido screamed for some action. Thank God she and Kate were off to the Gold Coast for some single-girl fun.

'I don't reckon anyone will be coming to town today Oscar,' Bonnie said to her old ginger cat who slept soundly underneath the bench.

'There's probably no point in dusting either.' She scraped a finger through the thick layer of red dust that dulled the polished wooden bench. Oscar opened one eye in annoyance, then stood up before turning his back to her.

'Fine. Ignore me then!' Bonnie harrumphed as her phone rang. The name flashing on her screen was cause for excitement.

'Kate, where have you been? I've been calling.'

'Hi Bon, jury service. So boring, but I couldn't get out of it.' Kate had her whiny tone on. 'How's Wingillie?'

Bonnie patted Oscar who'd jumped up on the bench for attention. 'Oh, you know dusty, hot, no single men.'

'Bonnie, you wanted the adventure of being in an outback town, remember?' Kate admonished.

Bonnie remembered, all right. Depressed and disheartened with city life, she'd jumped at the chance a year ago to purchase the general store in Wingillie, dreaming of handsome cowboys, country music, making jams and picnics. The reality was dusty buildings, stinky road-trains, old men and hot, endless days.

'I know, I love it, it's just not …'

'Not the same as those racy romances you read?'

Kate knew her so well. None-the-less there wasn't anything that could tear Bonnie away from those stories. She dreamed of a white knight rushing in and sweeping her off her feet, or even better a hot sexy cowboy showing her a good time.

'All set for this weekend?' Bonnie asked hopefully, looking longingly at the plane ticket pinned to her notice board so she wouldn't lose it. She really needed a girl's weekend with her friend—drinking cocktails, girl talk, dancing and maybe a hot one-night stand.

'Um, sorry.'

'No. Kate, not again. What's the excuse this time?' Bonnie tried to push away the prickle of resentment.

'It's Rob,' Kate whispered and Bonnie asked her to repeat it.

'Rob?' Bonnie squeaked in disbelief. 'The Rob who dumped you for the fling with a backpacker?'

'Yes, that's the Rob.'

'Are you mad?' Bonnie asked standing up and shaking her leg as pins and needles spasmed around her foot.

'I knew you'd be like this.'

'Like this? What do you mean, like this?' Bonnie yelled, an angry heat rushing to her head. 'You mean I'm not supposed to disagree with you? Tell you what I think?'

Yes, Bonnie had a weakness for romance novels, but Kate was defenceless against jerks and friends told each other the truth.

'I can't believe you, Kate. Blowing me off for him?'

'I'm really sorry, Bon. What could I do? He's been so lovely—' Bonnie ended the call and screamed. She wouldn't subject herself to the justification rolling off Kate's tongue. It'd be bull-dust. More bull-dust than was flying through the main street of Wingillie.

She paced the floor behind the bench. She could just go on her own; she was a strong independent woman. Her pace slowed. Except she absolutely hated going to night-clubs on her own.

She screamed, kicking at the closest target—a small paper bin. It spun clockwise across the linoleum floor, spilling screwed-up paper in its wake.

Oscar pinned back his ears, stretched, gave her a foul look and stalked to his biscuit tray.

The doorbell for her back door sounded.

She glanced at the clock and sighed. It would be Howard with the mail delivery. Work called her back to reality. She slumped her shoulders, and sipped some cool water before she trudged to the door, disappointment weighing her down. She'd have to get a credit on her ticket —again.

She opened the door wedging a foot in the corner as her sweet old delivery man entered. 'Hey, Howard. Quick get in here before you bring all of the desert with you.'

'Hey there Miss Bonnie.' Howard said his rheumy eyes twinkling with the mischief of a three-year-old. 'Only got one bag of mail today.'

'Excellent.' Bonnie groaned inwardly. In her current mood having less to do wasn't ideal.

'Oh, there's this one parcel—the wrapping is ripped. I can't see who it's addressed to.' He handed her a box. The brown wrapping had torn, revealing a clear, hard plastic case. She frowned and turned it over. No return address. The handwriting on the front read. *To*—name was missing due to the tear—*Care of the Wingillie Post Office, Wingillie QLD.*

She turned the parcel over again and squinted inside the plastic case. Howard stopped whistling as he dumped the mail-bag near her sorting bench. 'You're not looking inside people's parcels are you Miss Bonnie?'

She placed the box on her bench quickly turning her back on it. 'Of course I'm not, Howard. That would be an offence. Tampering with mail.'

Howard winked at her and recommenced his whistling.

Cheeky old bugger! She smiled bit at his retreating back.

'You know,' he said, 'there was a mystery box similar to that one years ago. Sat here in the post office for almost twenty years.'

Bonnie's ears pricked at this. She straightened and crossed her arms. 'Oh, and what happened?'

Howard turned and gazed at her. He paused seemingly for the full effect, and then launched into his story.

'Well, this bloke turns up, asking for the package see? And Mary, who had the post office before you, she couldn't believe it. They'd had bets on it at the pub. The odds were that no one would ever turn up to get it and here was this bloke. Very handsome, if I remember rightly.'

Bonnie leaned forward her hands under her chin, completely engrossed in Howard's story.

He stopped talking and smiled at her.

'Then what happened, Howard?' She stood up, frustrated. Why did Howard always drag his stories out?

'Then … nothing. I was pulling your leg. You believed me, though didn't you?'

He scuttled away, laughing as Bonnie threw a newspaper after him.

'Come on you, I'll make you a cuppa and a sandwich before you have to go.' Bonnie couldn't help but laugh. At least he'd cheered her up after Kate's downer.

A couple of hours later Bonnie waved Howard off.

'See you next week!'

She covered her eyes as the dust pelted around the door. Shutting it quickly, she stomped her feet at the mat and shook the particles of dirt from her dark hair. She'd have a long soak in a cold tub tonight. With a glass of something alcoholic and sparkling. Whatever she could get at the pub. She wouldn't let Kate ruin her weekend. She'd treat herself to an at-home spa. And she'd enjoy the new novel that had just arrived for her in the mail the newest regency from her favourite author, *The Masked Rogue.*

She looked longingly at the cover that featured a shirtless, tanned man wearing a black mask, and then grabbed some batteries off the shelf for her vibrator. Might as well go the whole hog. A long soak, shave her legs, a glass of bubbles, read her romance novel, followed by multiple orgasms. It'd been ages since she'd treated herself to some pleasure. She'd come back to work on Monday revived and relaxed. Stuff Kate and Rob—they deserved each other. At least a vibrator didn't break your heart.

She stood after putting the packet of triple A's in her bag and her gaze fell on the torn parcel.

Intrigued she picked it up and shook it gently. Paper rustled inside. It wasn't very heavy, under two hundred grams according to the postage sticker. She held it up to the light, tilting it to illuminate the contents. Inside, something glittered.

Her heart began to race. She couldn't open it? Could she? What if it accidentally tore, just a teensy bit more?

Looking around for something sharp, she grabbed a ruler and snagged the corner of it in the tear, then with a slight pull, the tear became bigger.

A loud crash outside caused her to jump.

She giggled when she saw her store sign banging at the front door. She ducked out to retrieve it, closing her eyes against the dust and leaves that swarmed around her. Back inside, she looked up at the clock. Almost four, and there'd been no-one all day. The likelihood of someone wanting groceries or postage now was next to impossible, so she locked the door.

In confusion, she noticed the parcel had disappeared from where she'd left it. She looked to Oscar who was absently cleaning a paw, then she saw a line of dust and leaves along the floor. The wind must've blown the parcel from where it had sat.

She jumped up to peer over the large wooden bench. The parcel lay on its side, the brown wrapping torn even more. As she rounded the bench, the contents became clear and she gasped.

No. Was someone playing a joke on her? Had Howard known about her book and was he now teasing her? The cheeky bugger that must be it. He'd set her up!

She returned the plastic box to the bench, opened the lid, and lifted out an exquisite hand-beaded masquerade mask made of black velvet. Strangely similar in style to the mask on her new romance novel.

She held it up to cover her eyes and turned to admire herself in the wall mirror. Fine, black satin ribbons hung softly from the sides. She reached up and tied them, securing the mask in place.

With a tilt of her head, she smiled.

Sexy.

The beads gleamed under the lights, twinkling as she arched her head. Her cheeks flushed a light shade of pink, matching her full lips, which she smacked together, blowing herself a kiss. Her dark hair framed her face and fell like a shimmering curtain over her shoulders. Her pale skin and dark eyes created a mysterious wanton look as she pulled various romance novel poses.

A sudden banging on the front door brought her back to reality with a jolt. She turned to see a tall man outside. He waved at her, gesturing towards the lock. Embarrassed and hoping he hadn't seen her posing, she whipped off the mask, placed it in its box and rushed to the door.

'I'm so sorry, I didn't expect anyone to be out in this …'

Her words died as the man stepped through the door. It was his scent that she noticed first. He smelled … expensive. She hadn't smelled anything that good outside of Myer's men's fragrance department.

Second, she noticed his height. He towered over her. She allowed her gaze to wander up his toned body, her stomach flipping, as a warmness filled her core, making her clit tingle. Then his eyes. Dark blue. Penetrating. She felt as if he could read her thoughts, and at that moment the thought of penetration was having a field day between her legs. Her clit throbbed, and she swallowed scrambling away.

'Ah, sorry, what can I do for you?' she finally managed, groaning when her voice squeaked.

He paced slowly towards her. She was reminded instantly of Oscar and how he stalked the sparrows in the yard. He proffered his hand, and she noticed he wasn't a farmer. No one had manicures in the outback.

Trembling, she took his hand, jumping as a shot of electricity passed between them. He smiled, but remained still, holding her hand.

'Bonnie Wright, I presume?'

Bonnie felt sure she was going to faint. His voice was deep, with a timbre that told her he could fuck her all night and all day if she asked.

Her voice shook but she managed to answer 'Yes?'

He let go of her hand. 'Bonnie, my name is Dale Blakley. I'm a friend of Kate's'

Kate? How did Kate know this Adonis and why hadn't she ever mentioned him before? He continued as she hesitated, 'I know her through work.'

Bonnies mind scoured over her past conversations with Kate. Had there been a time when Kate had mentioned anyone who matched his description?

Ping! Two months ago, Kate mentioned meeting a guy at a work function. What were her exact words? Sexy with a capital S.E.X. She wasn't wrong. Was he a model? No. A photographer! That was it.

Bonnie swallowed and tried to smile through her taut nerves.

'So, what brings you to Wingillie?'

'I'm a photographer Bonnie.'

God, she could come from the way he said her name. He may as well have been licking the juices off her clit. She shivered at the erotic image and hoped her couldn't actually read her mind.

'Actually,' he said, leaning casually against the bench, 'I've just seen something, that I'd love to photograph?'

Her nipples hardened as he stared at her, his gaze lowering slowly to her breasts then back to her eyes.

'Oh, something on the way into town?' she said tilting her head and pressing her breasts out further as though his stare would turn into lips and tongue.

'No.' He lifted a heated look back to her own. 'It's you … in that mask.' He gestured towards the black mask in the box.

Oh God. She wished a sinkhole would open up and swallow her. He'd seen her posing like a complete nut-job.

DALE ENJOYED WATCHING the many emotions that crossed her pretty face. When Kate had said her friend Bonnie was living in the outback, it had piqued his interest. Kate had babbled on about how Bonnie was into romance books, and again he was further intrigued. He was currently working on an exhibit titled 'Incongruous.' He travelled the country taking photos of people in odd situations. To his mind, a pretty young thing obsessed with romance novels and living in the outback would sit perfectly in his exhibition. It had still been a guess until he'd laid eyes on her five minutes ago. Watching her pretend and model had excited him. She'd been completely relaxed, comfortable in her skin and confident in her sexy poses. Sending the mask for her to discover was genius. It had been a big risk but it had paid off. Playing to what he'd guessed was her romantic imagination.

The remnant of his hard-on was still with him.

He wanted to photograph her naked now that he had seen her—but would she be up for that?

SILENCE ACCOMPANIED by bursts of the howling wind outside filled the general store as Bonnie coughed, her face heated, flushing from her chest upwards.

'I'm sorry can you please repeat that?'

'I asked, if I could photograph you naked?'

Bonnie laughed. 'God, I'm sorry. I thought you said naked. Naked. As in no clothes?'

He stared at her, a small serene smile lighting his face as he gazed at her. 'You're quite beautiful, you know. Completely unaware of the effect you have which makes you even more exquisite.'

Bonnie stepped behind the bench, leaving him on the other side. Her nerves tingled and she wanted to pinch herself. This wasn't the sort of thing that happened to her. She blinked rapidly. No, not asleep.

'I'm serious Bonnie. My photos are all class. I'll show you. Then you can decide. I'm staying at the pub. Come have a meal with me? Please, I promise you won't be disappointed.'

Bonnie looked at the familiar pub across the road, its cream weatherboards coated in a film of red dust. A couple of locals ventured outside, lighting cigarettes, squinting at the sun beers in hand. The wind had stopped, the dust had settled. This stranger had managed to change the feel of Wingillie in only five minutes.

She glanced at him and was filled with a desire so

strong and so bright. He was older than her, but only by five years maybe. This could be the fling she'd dreamed of. No promises, no regrets, but perhaps he would leave her lasting memories. And she'd have the photos to prove it.

What the hell? She was young, sexy and ready for adventure. And for the first time in a long while, Bonnie actually believed it.

THE MEAL AT THE PUB, interspersed with jibes from the old farmers who knew her, had actually been quite fun. Dale had played the part of an old friend come to town to catch up. But now as she followed him out to the rooms at the back of the pub, her nerves returned full-flight. Her body had been tingling since his arrival. Every slight touch from him was a massive turn-on. Honestly, she bet even a kiss on the forehead from him would make her orgasm.

He wriggled the key into the lock and turned it. Holding his arm along the door to keep it open he gestured, into the room.

'Ladies first?'

His wolfish grin sent tingles of excitement to her throbbing clit, the fabric of her dress teasing her sensitive nipples. God, she needed to calm down. But it had been a long time between men. Her trusty vibrator did the job, but she needed flesh and blood, throbbing and penetrating with heat and passion.

'Is it hot in here?' she asked fanning her flushed face with her hand. She'd worn a simple pink shift dress, flat sandals and no makeup—and had left her hair out.

He smiled and pressed the remote at the split system on the wall.

'There are other ways you could get cool, you know.' He left the sentence hanging as he turned to get his laptop.

Bonnie didn't think it was possible to be turned on any more than she was, but after those words, her imagination had her naked on his bed, her legs spread wide as he slipped his fingers inside her, caressing her clit with his thumb. She closed her eyes, her body swaying to the imaginary sensations.

'Bonnie?'

Oh God, he'd been talking and she'd been dreaming of him finger-fucking her.

'Did you want to see these photo's?' He sat sprawled in a chair, one arm casually along the desk, the other pulling a chair up for her.

She walked slowly, every step an intense agony of pleasure as the pressure increased between her legs. With a deep sigh she sat. He wrapped an arm around her chair, electricity fizzing between them as his arm touched her bare skin.

'So, here are some of the photos I've taken for the exhibit.'

She turned her attention to the laptop, trying to ignore his scent and closeness. Black and white images filled the screen. A ballet dancer at a funeral, a truck driver having makeup applied, an old woman at a school desk. The simple beauty of them made her sigh.

She turned her head; her nose almost touched his ear. When had he moved so close? He turned to look at her, his lips achingly near hers. 'So, what do you think?' His breath wisped across her skin. He reached a hand up to stroke her cheek. 'Will you do it?'

She grabbed his face and pressed her lips against his. She needed a release. It was time to be brave.

With a groan he pulled her tight against him, deepening the kiss. His tongue stroked hers and she pulled away desperate for a more intimate touch.

'Yes. I'll do it.' She was breathless with desire and at that moment she would have agreed to anything as long as it involved them both getting naked.

He smiled broadly; his eyes bright with passion. He lifted her easily. Carrying her to the bed he placed her down.

'Do you have the mask?' he asked, his voice low, causing a flush of moisture in her pussy.

She nodded breathless, and pointed to her bag.

He took a step as he unzipped his jeans. 'That's good because I want to fuck you while you wear it.'

She inhaled. This was really happening. The sexiest man she'd ever met was going to fuck her.

He held the mask towards her and then dropped it on the bed, 'But first your dress.' His jeans were undone, a tell-tale bulge between the zipper. Lust pounded through her. She wanted him. All of him. His fingers brushed her legs as he reached for the hem of her dress.

With the lightest of touches, he stripped her dress off over her head. She shivered, even though it was still warm. A low growl reverberated in his throat as he smiled.

'No underwear? Such a naughty surprise.' He growled cupping her breast in his hand and leaned in to take a nipple between his lips.

'Oh yes.' She pressed herself against him, eager to be touched, licked, kissed.

He kissed his way along her body to her pussy, then he lifted her leg and hooked it over his shoulder. He blew across her hot, engorged clit. She almost buckled and then with a single touch of his firm tongue, she vibrated in a white-hot burst.

He continued the erotic pressure of his warm pliable

tongue against her sensitive nub. His fingers slid between her folds and she gasped as he pushed his fingers inside her, his thumb caressing her soft lips. She arched against his hand. She wanted more, but she didn't want him to stop either. Gently pulling his silken hair, she held him close.

Don't stop.

He continued licking her as she met the rhythm of his fingers with tiny thrusts building up to an enticing cadence. She was going to come.

Bonnie gasped as he removed his hand slowly and stood, his gaze never leaving hers.

'You're so beautiful, but I don't want you to come yet.'

He lifted the mask and she held it against her face while he tied it gently behind her head. The weight of the mask changed her, gave her a confidence to be bold, desirable—someone else. She turned to look at him and then lay on the bed, spreading her legs wide in invitation.

'Exquisite.' he growled as he stripped off his jeans and his briefs. Tearing his black t-shirt over his head, he joined her on the bed.

She closed her eyes behind the mask, feeling seductive, sexy and wanton. She wanted him every way she could have him. The black mask gave her a sense of freedom, out-of-herself. She was living the life of a heroine in a romance novel.

She pushed him back onto the bed. His cock was ready —thick and erect. She knelt between his legs and licked across the head. He groaned and arched up into her, pushing himself inside her lips, his saltiness saturating her mouth and filling her with a passionate power. The power to give him pleasure, the power to take it as well. Tracing a finger along his hard length she squeezed a fist around him watching the ecstasy of her touch cross his face.

The heady pull of desire overcame her.

'Do you have a condom?'

He reached across and grabbed his jeans producing a foil packet from the pocket. He tore it open and rolled the condom over his length. Her breath hitched at how erotic it was to see him touching himself.

She straddled his hips and cock and slowly lowered herself, pressing her hands against smooth chest for balance. She pinched his nipples between her fingers and he released his breath in a hiss. Tightening her thighs against his, she relished the feel of his cock slowly filling her softness. She groaned her desire.

He smiled and grabbed her hips impaling himself inside her. She gasped as his balls slammed against her arse. He was so deliciously hard. She gripped his forearms and met his thrusts, and soon she couldn't take anymore. She reached a hand to her aching clit and stroked the sensitive bud until she finally came. Screaming her release, she tingled as her muscles contracted again and again around his cock.

Not long after he yelled her name and gave one final deep thrust. Then he pulled her down to him and kissed her. His tongue darted though her lips, and danced passionately with her own. He rained kisses along her throat, sucking the skin at her shoulder, causing her to break out in goose flesh. They quieted, satiated, heavy with satisfaction. The sound of their panted breaths filled the room, her perfume mingling with his aftershave, mixed with the musky smell of sex.

He rubbed his hand along her spine and she felt him harden again inside her. With a raised eyebrow she lifted her head to gaze at him.

'Ready for more?'

He nodded with a wide grin and flipped her onto her back. 'This time I'm in control!'

'FUCK, YOU'RE SO BEAUTIFUL'

His camera clicked and clacked as he moved from angle to angle, frame to frame. Dappled light from the gum trees danced all around as a flock of loud cockatoo's squawked their disapproval.

'That's it. Imagine I'm fucking you. Yeah, I'm in balls deep and you're loving it. Show me those wanton, sexy, blow-job eyes. That's it.' He crooned.

Bonnie could not remember a time when she'd felt more beautiful. He'd set up the photo shoot in the local dry creek bed. He'd had an enamel claw-foot bathtub brought down—God knows where he found it out here—and filled it with water and bubbles. Now she lay in it, with a romance novel and the black beaded mask on. The mask was now and forever more her favourite thing.

God the sex. It had been amazing. Her pussy still tingled in memory of last night, of the things they'd done. She changed her angle and posed with her lips pouted.

'Gorgeous. Give me some tongue, lick those lips like you're going down on me.'

She was already so aroused, and every word made her wetter. Bubbles preserved her modesty. No one other than Dale would see her naked today. He'd banned any bystanders not that anyone had been interested. Of course, they thought he was some artsy-type taking landscape photos—as they'd been led to believe.

Bonnie wondered about the other women he'd photographed. Had he seduced them as well? Not that she cared. She had no cause to feel jealous. She didn't love him. Well, not in that happily-ever-after way. But she loved how he made her feel. And she knew that there'd be more sex after the photo shoot. She could see his erection bulging in his jeans from her spot in the bath.

Blinking slowly, she blew him a kiss as he finished up declaring 'Well, that's a wrap!' He walked over to her and offered his hand as she stood. The bathwater ran across her body in bubbly rivulets. He shook his head with a heavy sigh and leaned in to kiss her.

As she stepped out onto the waiting mat, she guided his hands to her breasts. 'All that talk has me so horny. I think I need you to help me.' New, bold Bonnie wasn't afraid to be honest with a man, so forthright in declaring her desires. The mask—it must be magic.

He grabbed a fluffy towel wrapped it around her shoulders and grinned, winding his arms around her tightly.

'Bonnie Wright you're the best subject I've ever had the pleasure of photographing. Happy to fuck you whenever you need, just call and I'll be here.'

Feeling brave behind her mask she suggested, 'Well, let's make it regular. Once every two months. You can come here?'

She groaned at her boldness and held her breath.

He stroked the skin on her cheek, letting his hand drift down along her neck and shoulder toward her hardened nipples. He leaned in and sucked a hard, rosy nub into his mouth. She gasped as his teeth nipped her skin.

Massaging her breasts in his hands he returned his burning gaze to hers. 'You know what Bonnie. Promise you'll always wear that mask and you've got a deal.'

Bonnie squealed as he knelt in front of her and lifted her leg over his shoulder. As his tongue rolled over her clit, she closed her eyes. He mightn't be a knight in shining armour carrying her away from Wingillie on his white horse, but he was giving her the best sex of her life and she'd never felt more desirable. For now, that was better than all the knights-in-waiting.

Bonnie twisted her fingers through his hair arching herself closer to him.

Besides, it was a woman's prerogative to choose her best-ever-after. Maybe Bonnie's didn't include a knight right now, but at this moment, it did include a mind-blowing orgasm.

Esther Jones and the Temple of the Moon

JOSIE BAKER

EGYPT, 1939

The last block of mudbrick wall groaned as Hans levered it away from the entrance of the ancient rammed-earth structure. Hot, stale air gusted out of the opening, instantly drying the sweat on Esther Jones's face. She glanced at her business partner. His expression mirrored her triumph. Even if it wasn't the lost tomb of Mehu, whatever they found inside would surely finance their continued search for the legendary treasure.

'After you,' Hans said with a gallant wave of his arm that belied his calculating expression.

She stepped past him, careful not to come into contact with any part of his body. An attractive man with dirty blond hair and warm brown eyes, the treasure-hunter was physically strong from heavy work, yet lean from their erratic diet. He would have been Esther's ideal companion, except theirs was a partnership built on a mutual goal, not trust, since the disappearance of their most profitable find. Esther dragged her gaze from his handsome face with renewed disenchantment. If they'd sold it to a private collector, the lapis lazuli and gold amulet would have ensured a life of comfort for them both. Obviously, half its worth was not enough for Hans. What she couldn't comprehend was why he hadn't already disappeared. Was he continuing their alliance to assuage her suspicion, until he found the most lucrative buyer for the amulet? Or was he worried she'd go on to find Mehu's tomb without him?

'Will you bring the torches?' Esther asked, and, impatient to start, strode into the inky darkness. After a few steps, she bumped into a large, squared-off stone as high as her hips. The approaching torchlight revealed an altar. A temple, then, not a tomb. *Damn.*

'Another goose chase?' Hans explored the unadorned walls and floor of the small room with the beam of his torch. After five days of travelling to yet another new location, they'd stumbled upon the blocked entrance of the undocumented site and dared to hope they'd discovered the treasure-hunter's Holy Grail.

'It's a *wild* goose chase. And it may not be Mehu, but beggars can't be choosers,' Esther replied sharply. Without the funds from the sale of the amulet, they were dead broke.

She glanced at the scattering of artefacts and sighed. The absence of rich grave goods from a tomb find was disappointing, but hopefully what they *had* found would fund their search for a few more months at least.

With dusk approaching and a long way to travel back to civilisation, they had no time to study what they packed. Once the small crates were strapped to the camels, they set off through the night, the sand beneath their feet lit by an nearly full moon.

By mid-morning, they arrived at the hotel where they'd stayed the week before. Poorly built almost one hundred years earlier, it was the only place in the settlement they could afford. Wearily, they unloaded their baggage, splitting the boxes between their two rooms. Esther ensured the box she'd marked with an indistinguishable cross in charcoal went to hers. Her mind had been on the contents since the moment she'd found it.

When she'd picked up the linen-wrapped bundle in the dim light of the temple, it had called to her, a honey-smooth voice inside her head intoning words she didn't recognise. Captivated, her fingertips buzzing from the strange energy the object emitted, she'd unwrapped the age-thinned fabric. The eyeholes of the ritual mask inside seemed to stare into her soul. Shaken and intrigued, she'd packed it away before Hans noticed her interest.

In her room, Esther placed the box one from the top, hiding the cross against the wall, then joined Hans in what passed for the dining room. Weak with fatigue, they broke their fast with fresh figs, bread and honey before collapsing in their separate beds.

Even naked, the heat made sleep restless. Woken from dreams of flickering torchlight and a bronze moon filling the sky, Esther tried to orientate herself. An eerie orange light streamed through the broken blinds. The last of the sun's rays painted the flimsy walls with gold, and through the gaps in the plaster, she caught glimpses of Hans gathering his clothes. A rattle and click as he—uselessly—locked his door. Now alert, she tracked his footfalls down the hallway to the communal shower room. *Not disappearing, then. Not yet.*

In a flash Esther was out of bed with the marked box open. She carried the linen-wrapped mask to the window, where, in a shaft of late afternoon light, she could finally see it clearly. She gasped with awe at the craftsmanship, the feline-shaped eyeholes, nose and ears. In the years she'd spent travelling as an archaeologist with her aunt and uncle, and recently as a treasure-hunter, she'd never seen anything fashioned so intricately from hair, as if each strand were individually woven.

There was no question it was museum quality, undamaged as it was, and if crafted of human hair—not mane or tail—its sale would finance their quest for years. Or her retirement if she kept it for herself.

The muffled sound of Hans showering stopped and she hurried back to the boxes, afraid he would see her through the gaps when he returned to his room. Mask in one hand, linen in the other, she tried not to think of her business partner naked, droplets of water rolling over his body. The squeak of the shower door told her time was running out, but she was unable to put the mask away. It seemed to cling to her hands, entreating her to claim it as her own.

She turned the mask and, mesmerised by a glimpse of mother-of-pearl, brought it close to her face. As the eyes came closer and she looked through the openings, a wave of desire surged through her from her fingers to her toes. Like lightning, awareness raced over her skin, sensitising her lips. The caress of a thousand finger tips cascaded over her breasts, teasing her nipples and flowing over from her abdomen to her sex.

The knock on her door halted further progress of the mask towards her face. Esther glanced at the door, breaking the connection.

Slipping the mask beneath her bed sheets and throwing on her robe, she opened the door to find Hans, bare-chested and towelling his shower-darkened hair. She'd seen him shirtless before, his biceps and pecs taut and tanned, but she'd never seen him like this. He looked like a bronze statue, glowing in the rays of the dying sun.

'It's too hot to sleep longer. I'm going downstairs for a drink, or shall I bring something up to share?'

4333 YEARS EARLIER …

Hesta sat cross-legged as she worked, her lips moving with silent spells as she wove the ceremonial mask.

As high priestess of the temple to the cat goddess, she wove magic with her sacred hair. With each straight black strand, Hesta wove stamina and prolificacy for the high priest. Normally, corn husks would be used, but Setka's arrogance forced her to extremes.

Unlike the priestesses, the high priest was out of touch with the village he served, ignorant of the extent of their escalating hardship—the shortage of fish from the river, and the absence of inundation which had led to the failure of crops. Just the week before, another child stillborn to a mother of two, and a sacred oryx dead in the prime of life.

At Hesta's request, the most powerful members of the tribe had met prior to the ceremonial isolation period. She had suggested the need for an extraordinary fertility ritual, but Setka refused, adamant the regular ritual would suffice to please their gods.

Hesta refused to stand by and watch her people suffer further. Setka's power was as precious as her own, and as fleeting. With every tool at her disposal, she would amplify their combined power. If the modified ritual she'd prepared failed, their tribe would not survive another year.

With the exterior of the mask completed, Hesta stood and stretched. She ignored the desolation that clawed at her chest at the absence of the familiar weight, the silken caress against her back, the tickle against her buttocks. By sacrificing her hair, the most potent of her magic, she also sacrificed the position she was born to and a lifetime of training. Everything she held dear, offered to the gods for the benefit of the village.

Hesta walked to the alter and knelt to retrieve the casket of nacre stored beneath. Harvested from the sacred bay in the Red Sea, the mother-of-pearl, when inlaid into the lining of the mask using precise charms, would guide the high priest to take a physical rather than symbolic role in the ceremony.

Then, with the mask in place, she would embody the black cat goddess and offer her womb as a welcoming receptacle.

WITH THE DAWN, Hesta broke her three-day fast and bathed before painting the entire surface of her flawless skin with powdered azurite. Only a little was needed to enhance the magic of the moon, but she wasn't taking any chances.

Chanting a prayer of thanks to the goddess, she nestled the temple's sacred emerald in her navel, securing it with beeswax. The gem, usually set into the centre of the altar, would guarantee her fertility.

Bloated and bronze, the full moon bulged above the horizon by the time Hesta pulled on the black robe and hood and stepped out of the temple of the cat goddess. With her eight priestesses pacing behind, she walked the ceremonial way through the village, carrying before her the elixir she'd prepared for the ceremony. The entire village lined the path, throwing whatever leaves and petals could be found still living. Old men and women, hoping for a few last years of ease; adults, praying for their children's health and survival; children, some so young they hadn't known better times.

Yes, Hesta thought, *the sacrifice was worth it.*

The procession paced parallel to the dying river to the

bull god's temple. Hesta entered, her silver-blue skin and shorn hair hidden beneath her robe.

As her priestesses filed inside, Hesta allowed herself the indulgence of studying the high priest. Setka waited, motionless and regal at the head of his altar, polished skin tawny against the white cape thrown back from his shoulders, naked but for a white loincloth. Many times, she had imagined touching his slim, sculpted body, and fantasised about the pleasure they might find together.

Tonight, her goddess would have his power, and Hesta would have *him*.

Positioned in a circle around the altar stone, the priestesses began to chant, gathering power and inviting the presence of the goddess. Setka, shaved and oiled, glinted in the flickering light, intoning a complementary monosyllabic *ooom* to accompany the women's voices.

Hesta remained standing to offer him the elixir, her first deviation from the annual ritual. She looked him in the eye, challenging him to accept her as an equal.

He acknowledged the deviation with narrowed eyes but accepted the cup, drinking half the contents.

Hesta threw off her robe. Despite his self-possession, the high priest gasped to see her head shorn. He had known Hesta since she was initiated as priestess and had never seen her so exposed. Gathering his composure, he offered the chalice back to her, bowing his head to show reverence for the beauty of the goddess. Hesta threw back the bitter potion, tossed the dish hard to break it and approached the alter.

Feeling his gaze on her back like a physical caress, she moved backwards up the steps and lay on the altar. She stretched out on a bed of grain from the last successful harvest, three years past, and looked up at Setka. He seemed to swell in size, standing taller, muscles firmer, skin luminescent. Pinning Hesta with his gaze, he threw off his cape and picked up the ritual jug of his temple, intoning the prayer to transform the milk of lettuce into the bull god's seed.

Continuing her role, Hesta began to chant, not the traditional words of the fertility ritual, but the ones she had used to imbue the mask with power. Words to override twenty years of the high priest's training.

If he touched her, she would know she had him.

The priest frowned, but intoned the words the ritual demanded of him, appealing to the bull god to join his power with that of the goddess to bring fertility to the village.

The tension in Hesta's body receded, replaced with shivers of anticipation. Whether by choice or enchantment, the priest had committed to the ritual. Surely, if he were going to rebel, he would not have invited his god to the party?

Setka's voice took on a depth not heard in previous rituals, as if the bull god were present in more than spirit, lured by the promise of the illicit.

The voices of the priest and the nine priestesses halted, the sudden silence ringing with power. Hesta closed her eyes, praying silently. Starting at her forehead, the priest god anointed her with milk from the jug, dribbling it over her flesh until it flowed from her body to soak the grain beneath her—its seed would be sown at dawn.

At the touch of his fingers on her forehead, Hesta's eyelids flashed open, and she watched his gaze follow the movement of his fingers on her flesh. From cheeks to lips, neck to chest, circling breasts and the sacred stone nestled in her navel, the combination of his gaze and the pressure of his touch ignited a trail of awareness. With each stroke of his fingers, pleasure rippled over her flesh, enhancing the power of her spell.

When the cool liquid flowed over the mound of her yoni and between her lips, with the touch of the god following in its wake, she struggled not to writhe with need. Instead, she drew the magic inside, gathering it in her womb. By the time the god's anointment reached the soles of her feet, she trembled with a power she could barely contain. It was time to release her pleasure as fertility for the tribe.

The words that bubbled from her lips and the timbre of her voice were unfamiliar to her ears. Words from the goddess to her consort.

Setka smashed the now empty jug on the earth and ascended the steps to the top. With a twitch of the knot, he unfurled his loincloth and the god's instrument sprang free.

His body eclipsed the flare of the torches, the light visible only as an aura around him, and the bull god lowered himself over her. Hesta gasped as impaled her with his phallus, her sex burning with the touch of the god, need pulsing through her body. The powdered beetle she'd added to the potion to engorge his penis and increase Setka's stamina, also increased her sensitivity.

The priestess's chant increased, driving his rhythm as the god took his pleasure. The flare of ecstasy when he spilled his seed inside her nearly blinded her, and her consciousness turned inward to the spark of life that lit inside her womb.

When Hesta became aware enough to open her eyes, all was dark, the torches extinguished by the rush of power as the god left. Her attendants were still, pale ghosts around the wall.

With his god gone, Setka appeared startled, still moving inside her, uncertainly.

But it was not over.

The god had taken his pleasure and left him, but Setka was still hard. The momentary realisation he had sacrificed his celibacy and committed an act that would cost his position as high priest evaporated with the return of sensation. The fantasies he'd spent years resisting could not have prepared him for the reality of thrusting into the woman he had been unable to banish from his dreams. So intense was the experience, he wondered if it would finish him; his body unable to contain the escalating pleasure.

As the priestesses relit the torches, their chants increasing in tempo with his thrusts, he gazed down at Hesta. His ecstasy was reflected in her beautiful face, the mixture of milk from the oblation and azurite smeared across her flesh, and on his. At the approach of his climax, he obeyed the urge to touch his lips to hers, to possess her mouth as well as her yoni. At the touch of her tongue against his, pleasure exploded through him and the clenching of her muscles around his phallus drove his rapture higher still.

'Hesta,' Setka groaned in her ear, not the voice of the god, or the high priest, but the man who loved her.

EGYPT, 1939

With Hans downstairs, Esther sat on the bed and rummaged through her knapsack looking for the jewellers' loupe. Human hair had a scale-type cuticle, but would it be visible under the magnifier, and would it look any different from other fibres?

She pulled out an alabaster bottle of musk oil she'd bought months ago but never worn. Taking out the stopper, she sniffed, inhaling sensuality and lust. Esther replaced the stopper and placed the bottle on the bedside table. The woman at the bazaar had promised the pheromones were an aphrodisiac, but Esther had resisted the temptation to try it out.

Returning to her search, she could tell the magnifying lens wasn't inside its leather pouch as soon as she lifted it. Something else was, something larger and heavier.

The amulet!

Her head spun with sudden relief. *It wasn't lost, and Hans didn't steal it.*

She remembered now—she'd accidentally dropped a casket lid on the lens, crushing it, but had forgotten in the excitement of the discovery of the Pharaoh's amulet. And later that night, she'd almost lost her partner.

Hans's knock jolted Esther from her memories. She dropped the pouch into her robe pocket and opened the door. He'd thrown on a linen shirt, but left it unbuttoned over shorts, his skin tan against the startling white fabric. He carried half a dozen bottles of beer wrapped in wet rags to keep them cool.

'Come in.' Esther closed the door behind him, nerves churning the meagre contents of her stomach. She'd suspected him of cheating her of her share, viewed his every action with suspicion since the amulet disappeared. She'd judged him unfairly and now it was time to come clean.

Hans put the bottles down on a crate and unwrapped one, offering it to her.

'Remember the night you fell from the first floor of the hostel in Hakkhor?' She accepted the beer, her eyes on the floor.

The night they'd found the ancient lapis lazuli amulet. They'd celebrated, the bottle of whisky they'd shared melting her resolve until she'd decided she would give in to the attraction she'd fought every day they'd worked together.

They'd been sitting side by side on the handrail when she'd felt him lose his balance. Time had slowed as if in a nightmare. She'd reached for him, but she'd been clumsy, hadn't got a proper grip on his forearm. She could still see the shock on his face when he'd realised he would fall.

Esther took a swig of the sharp beer, trying to wash away the image of Hans, motionless on the hard-packed sand. After a night in hospital and a day resting, they'd returned to their search for Mehu's tomb, the trust between them in tatters.

His face tightened with suspicion. 'I remember.'

Did he think she hadn't tried to stop his fall? Or worse, did he think she'd stolen the amulet then got him tipsy and nudged him off balance to prevent him finding out?

'The night I thought I'd lost you.' She didn't try to fight the tears that flooded her eyes, no longer afraid to let him hear the emotion in her voice. Their relationship, even with the tension of the last two months, was the closest she'd come to having family since the deaths of her aunt and uncle. It scared her to realise she'd let her suspicion ruin what could have been a partnership in every sense of the word.

Hans tilted his head with query, his expression softening. He cupped her face in his calloused hand. Esther stepped forward, pressing her cheek into his palm and looked up into the face of her beloved. With a groan, he lowered his lips to hers and wrapped his arm behind her to pull her close. The feel of his hard body pressed against hers stole her breath. It felt like an exquisite dream and she wanted to lose herself in it, but she needed to tell him first.

She pulled her lips from his, her body crying out at being cheated of what it most craved.

'The amulet is not lost.' Esther braced her hands against his chest when Hans tried to resume their kiss. 'Remember the day we found it?'

'Yes,' Hans said, unconcerned, and slid his fingers over her neck into her hair, sending tingles over her scalp and stealing her ability to think.

Esther bit her lip, the sting helping her to focus. 'I put it in the leather pouch we used to store the magnifying lens in, to keep it safe. I forgot, with the shock of your accident. But I found it.'

Hans released her and she stepped back, taking the pouch from her pocket and handing it to him. She watched his eyes widen with wonder as he pulled out the Eye of Horus.

'I thought I would never see it again,' he said and shook his head. 'I thought it was only a matter of time before I never saw *you* again.' He looked up and she realised the warmth in his eyes had nothing to do with their colour, but his feelings. Her body with heat. Even though he'd suspected her, he'd never stopped looking at her like that.

'You thought I took it.'

'It was the logical explanation.' He shrugged with a rueful smile.

'You would have let me leave with it.'

'I would have let you take it, yes.'

Esther couldn't find the words, couldn't have talked through the tightness in her chest. She didn't need to ask why. For the same reason she would have let him have the amulet. Because she loved him.

It was time to show him the mask.

'I found something important, in one of the boxes in my room.' What had she been thinking, not showing him sooner?

Esther pulled back her sheets to reveal the linen-wrapped package.

Hans moved forward, his face an emotionless mask. Too late, she realised how suspicious it looked, hiding an artefact in her bed. Just when she'd regained his trust. *Damn it!*

'It was calling to me.' A pathetic explanation, even to her own ears. 'Please understand, I was hesitant to show it to you.'

He placed the amulet on the bedside table and bent to pick up the linen-wrapped package. 'You didn't trust *me*. You thought *I'd* taken the amulet?'

'Yes,' Esther admitted.

He plunged his free hand into his pocket, pulled out a green gem the size of a flattened grape and placed in her palm.

'I suppose that makes us even, yes?' One side of his mouth turned up in a half-smile.

'I guess it does.' Esther grinned back, her stomach flipping at the promises in his eyes. He picked up the package and she watched his face as he unwrapped the mask, turning it this way and that to study it.

'This is priceless. And very powerful.' He shook his head in wonder and looked up at her. 'It was made for a woman's face.' He lifted the mask, cradled in his two hands, like a ceremonial offering.

'Maybe too powerful for the uninitiated?' Conflict held her immobile. Her entire being was drawn forward, but her mind told her everything about the situation was dangerous. An ancient ritual mask and the man she yearned for.

'I'm willing to take the risk, if you are.' His words hinted at more than exploring ancient magic together.

As she stepped towards him, he raised the mask level

with her eyes, so the mother-of-pearl framed her vision of him. An aura of luminescence flared around him and a growing power pulsed with the blood through her veins. Her nipples and sex tingled, an irresistible call, a promise that whatever the mask offered, it would be worth any sacrifice to experience. With him.

She walked forward until her face fitted to the mask. As the cool shell made contact, it seemed to mould to her, a vacuum between her damp skin and the slightly gritty surface of the nacre. Sensation exploded through her body and her lips began to move of their own volition, her voice intoning words she'd never heard. Untying her robe, she dropped it to the floor, offering her body to the god she saw through the mask.

He stepped forward, eyes blazing, seeming to follow commands only he could hear. He shrugged off his shirt, pulled the tie of the drawstring and stepped out of his shorts. Walking over to the narrow bed, he lay back, arms and legs outstretched in offering.

Esther nestled the emerald in her navel, picked up the oil bottle from the bedside table and knelt on the bed, straddling his hips. Taking out the stopper, she tilted the bottle over him. Oil dripped onto his chest, over his stomach, the scent of the musk enflaming her senses.

Beneath her, Hans's penis twitched for her touch. Delicious tension built in her abdomen as she dribbled the oil down the shaft, then stroked him, coating her palm with musk. Placing the bottle beside the bed, Esther repeated the process with her other hand while she anointed her breast with the oil. She pinched her nipple and a dart of pleasure speared through to her. Chasing the sensation, she rubbed her oil-coated fingers over her clit, and lowered herself onto his erection.

Instinctively, she moved over her lover, each thrust raw

and demanding, drawing his essence inside. Pleasure radiated out from the point of their union, filling them until they relinquished all control and conscious thought, their movements unrestrained, primitive.

Her orgasm rippled outward from her sex, through her limbs, until her entire body pulsed with pleasure and she cried out. Shaken from her trance, she looked down at her lover. His cock was still rigid inside her, but it was not Hans looking back at her.

With an effort, she pulled the mask away and dropped it to the floor. Although his eyes wandered over her face, Hans seemed lost. Taking his face in her hands, she pressed her mouth to his unresponsive lips. She persevered, moving her lips in time to the slow roll of her hips, begging him to come back to her even as the resurging pleasure of their coupling lured her to abandon her efforts.

With a groan, he slid his hand beneath her hair and pulled her face closer, crushing her lips to his, while his movements became smooth and fast beneath her.

Tears gathered in her eyes. He had returned to her.

Gasping, he released her lips and looked down at their bodies. The sight of Esther, naked, moving on his cock and the exquisite feeling of being inside her triggered his climax. His body tensed and arched beneath her, his gaze locked with hers as Hans gave himself to her.

SIX MONTHS LATER …

'It was a brilliant idea to donate the mask to the fertility clinic. But what will we do with the amulet? Sell it to a collector?' Esther placed her glass of iced tea on the coffee table, and transferred her gaze from the azure blue of the ocean to Hans. The small villa they'd rented was the closest place to a home she could remember.

Hans had just returned from the capital to collect the final payment for the emerald. Sitting forward in the easy-chair that matched her own, the breeze ruffling his dark blond hair, he picked up the leather pouch from the coffee table and stood.

'I have the ideal place for it,' he said and walked behind Esther. Taking the amulet on its leather thong from the pouch, he placed it over her head. 'It symbolises my commitment to you. It belongs with us.'

He came around and crouched beside her chair, spreading his palm over her swollen belly, and felt their child move in response to his voice and his touch.

'So, you're not going anywhere?' Esther asked, teasing, and placed one hand over his, the other on his cheek. The ritual they'd shared committed their flesh; the baby they'd created bound their souls.

'I'm not going anywhere without you. And her.'

4314 YEARS EARLIER …

Hesta watched her daughter prepare, proud of the role she would soon play, her passage into womanhood ensuring the prosperity of the tribe. After weeks of prepa-ration and a lifetime of training, Esta, daughter of Hesta, wove a mask from her freshly shorn hair. Three nights hence, the full moon would rise and Hesta's daughter—born of the bull god—would paint her skin with powdered azurite and don the cat mask.

The village had flourished since the modified ritual Hesta had instigated nineteen years earlier, and the elders had inscribed it as law. The daughter born of the sacred ceremony had dedicated her first eighteen years to prepare for the day she would enact her own ceremony to ensure the success of the village.

Hesta's work was almost done. Four days hence, she would finally leave the temple of the cat goddess, free to spend the remainder of her days with her consort, Setka. Free to enact their own rituals of love.

One-Night Stand-In

SUZIE JAY

'I'M GOING home to bed. If you value your jobs, you will not disturb me.' Penelope tucked her shoulder-length black hair behind her ear and reached for her coat. Would this head cold never go away?

'Ma'am, you have the children's charity event tonight.'

Penelope spun to see who had dared speak. Her dark eyes drilled into Albert when she saw him skulking in the corner.

'Albert, if you're going to take it upon yourself to attempt to order me around, I suggest you stand up straight and, at the very least, say it with some conviction.' She slipped on her coat and shoved her hands on her hips. 'Well, Albert? Do you have something to say?'

'I … I think it would be bad manners if you didn't show up. The business can't afford another public pillory.'

Albert tilted his chin and Penelope fought back the urge to laugh. Pathetic little man, thinking he could stand up to her.

'Your sensitive nature may not be able to bear another media attack, but my company and I can take anything anyone cares to dish out. Now, contrary to popular opinion, this is not an Alcoholics Anonymous meeting. You don't all get to have a say.' She dabbed at her nose with a tissue before tossing it in the bin. 'On that note, good afternoon.'

She strode to the door.

'But ma'am, it's for children. *Please*. We could do with some good press.'

Albert was at it again. Following behind her like some hungry rodent hoping to be thrown some crumbs.

She glared at him, her eyes fighting his. He looked away as she'd known he would. 'Send a replacement. The invitation is in the top drawer of my desk.'

'WE CAN'T JUST SEND anyone. It's important we're able to convincingly pass off whoever goes as Penelope.' Albert paced the office.

'This is ridiculous. If she doesn't care about her company, why should we?' Bethany snapped.

'It's her company, but our jobs are at stake,' Emma spoke up. A rare occurrence. An ex-boyfriend once told her she should wear grey so she could completely blend into the wallpaper. As much as it was intended to be an insult, Emma thought of it more as a life goal. If she could get through an entire day without people noticing her, it was a great day in her book.

Albert scurried over to her and looked her up and down.

'Exactly,' he agreed. 'And you strike an uncanny resemblance to Ms Penelope.'

Emma's face burned instantly. She wrapped her cardigan tighter around herself. 'I don't know about that.'

Albert smiled. 'Only in looks my dear. Not at all in personality.'

Emma *wished* she'd worn grey. 'I don't think I have the confidence to pull it off.'

It was a futile attempt. She could see the excitement buzzing around the room, gaining momentum like an out-of-control boulder rolling down a cliff.

'Nonsense,' Albert interjected. 'You're a touch short, so you'll have to wear heels, but other than that you're a perfect match.'

Bethany nodded her agreement. 'Yes, and you should avoid talking to too many people.'

Finally, something Emma was good at. 'But what if someone asks me something directly? The last thing I want is to seem stand-offish. That's what got the company into trouble the first time.'

Albert rubbed his greying stubbled jaw. 'You're her personal assistant, Emma. If you can't avoid them, be friendly, answer as vaguely as you can and then excuse yourself.'

'We really don't have time for this. The only people likely to approach are the charity organisers and Trent Whitaker. Surely you can handle Trent.' Bethany rolled her eyes.

At the mention of Trent's name, Emma's ears felt like they would sizzle right off her head until a pile of ash landed at her feet. As much as she knew she'd regret this, she couldn't say no to the opportunity to spend time with Trent. She lived for the moments he came to the office, and over the last eighteen months, her crush on him had developed into a full-blown infatuation.

'What will I wear?'

EMMA TUGGED at the hem of her dress to no avail. It sprang back up like a rubber band. She highly doubted Penelope would wear something this short and sparkly to a formal occasion. But who was she to argue? She knew nothing about fashion and was grateful when Bethany had taken control and brought around an outfit.

She had to admit, once her face had been covered with the masquerade mask, she did strike an uncanny resemblance to her boss with a similar small build and long dark hair. Having only just arrived inside the great hall, a group of three woman had called out to her, mistaking her for Penelope, and she'd let out a sigh of relief. This might just work.

Now she just had to find a quiet corner to hide in and take any chance she could to sneak into a few media group shots when the opportunities arose. It would serve as proof of Penelope's attendance. Then she'd drop a generous pledge, which Penelope could pay later, and make her exit.

The room buzzed with activity. People chatted and laughed while picking at the overstocked buffet. It was like a who's who of Melbourne's elite—they were the people who had big bucks to donate. Most were completely recognisable behind their flimsy lace-covered masks. After all, what would be the point of attending one of the biggest events of the year and donating a ridiculous amount of money if no one witnessed you doing it?

People danced in their glamourous ball gowns while half-heartedly holding their masks, practically at arm's-length in front of them by long sticks. If a tree falls in the forest and no one hears it fall, did it fall at all? Or whatever the saying was.

Emma made her way towards the back of the room to avoid the lighting from the oversized chandeliers. They sparkled, the light hitting the gold-trimmed decor perfectly, little beams of light reflected across the room in all directions. The last thing she wanted was to be illuminated like a Christmas tree.

She nodded to a waiter and he offered her a glass of champagne. Not normally one who drank a lot, now seemed like a great time for Emma to start. She needed the courage. With glass in hand, she made a bee-line for the back corner, stopping once or twice to pop into photos being taken by the society photographers.

Time dragged. It felt like she'd entered the ballroom hours ago, but a quick check of her phone told her only thirty minutes had passed. The place became more and more crowded and she glanced out the French doors that led onto a terrace and the beach beyond.

Surely she could slip out and sit with her feet in the water for a bit and rejoin the festivities later. These shoes Bethany had given her were cutting off her circulation. Emma could just imagine the relief it would be to take them off.

She stood and strode towards her escape.

'Leaving so soon?'

Emma didn't need to turn around to recognise the sound of honey melting over butter. It was Trent. A thrill ran along her spine and tingled every part of her on its way down.

Plastering on faux confidence, she smiled as she turned. His thick dark hair had been smoothed back and was more controlled than how he usually wore it. She liked it; it allowed her a better view of his chocolate eyes. He was dressed in a black tuxedo with a black shirt and tie. Without a doubt, this was the image women saw when they heard "tall, dark and handsome". He held a mask in his hand without so much as attempting to hide his identity. If she looked like him, she wouldn't cover it up either she supposed.

'Trent, darling, how lovely to see you.' That was the usual fake greeting Penelope gave a person she was preparing to stab in the back.

His dark eyebrows shot up as he failed to hide his shock.

'It's a nice surprise to see you here.' He leaned in and the smell of his musk aftershave surrounded her in a sea of fantasies. Trent kissed her on the cheek and her skin flared in response.

'It shouldn't be. I'd always intended on being here.' It was all she could do to tumble the words out when on the inside her nerves were playing havoc.

'Really? I wasn't aware you'd been invited.' He said it in a way that didn't sound at all like he was trying to one-up Penelope.

But why wouldn't Emma's boss be invited? She was invited to everything.

Trent's eyes drew over her and she felt an increase in her body heat the second they locked with hers.

'Of course I was invited,' was all she could think to say.

Trent's eyes scanned the room.

'Same stuffy people, discussing the same boring topics. I swear at times I'm stuck in my own nightmarish version of *Groundhog Day*.'

'Poor thing, being forced to hang out with the rich and famous.' The words slipped from her mouth before she'd even realised she'd thought them.

To Emma's relief, Trent stared into his drink and chuckled. 'It can get tedious at times, but on the odd occasion, things start to look up.'

He glanced at her, his chestnut eyes clashing with hers.

'How so?' Was it her imagination or was Trent Whitaker leaning in closer after each exchange?

'Well, just when I think I might pass away from boredom, there you are.' His face was mere inches from hers.

This wasn't at all ethical. She was here on business and he thought she was Penelope. She stepped back, hoping to break the spell, and adjusted her mask.

'You give me too much credit. Believe me, I'm as boring as everyone else.'

Her speech was flustered, and as much as she prayed he wouldn't notice, there was no denying the effect he had on her. It was as though a hundred butterflies tap danced their way around her stomach.

'Maybe even *more* boring,' she admitted, thinking how this was so unlike how she normally spent her Friday nights.

Unlike other women in their late twenties, she wasn't into the party scene. How could she expect a man of the world like Trent to understand the joy she got from dipping into a new book? But exploring the world through books was her favourite thing.

'I doubt I could find anything boring about you.' His gaze locked onto her eyes, and as much as she felt ridiculous in this bedazzled mask, she was thankful for the shield it provided.

She laughed. More to lighten the tension that swirled around them than at how ridiculous that statement would be if he knew the truth.

'I'll take that as a challenge. I could bore the pants off you in three seconds flat.'

Oh good God! Had she really said that out loud?

'You, me, no pants. I'm predicting that wouldn't be boring at all.'

He winked, and she shut her eyes while sinking down

through the floor and into the pits of hell. Only when she opened her eyes, she still stood in front of Trent with her mouth hanging open. And the heat she experienced was not from the devil's lair but from her own stupid, blushing face.

'I ... I didn't mean your pants would actually be removed. I meant ...' She let her voice trail away. Truth be told, she didn't know what she meant, and now she had the image of Trent standing in front of her without any pants.

Thank God he thinks I'm Penelope, was the only sane thought she could manage.

'As I said, not boring. Now, may I walk you to your car?' He held out his hand.

Emma ignored it. Her inner thighs already glistened with lust without physical contact tipping her over the edge.

'Oh, I wasn't leaving.' She dipped her head, indicating the sea beyond the terrace. 'Just thought I'd escape for a moment and take a walk on the beach. It's been a long day.' Her voice softened as she spoke, making her sound more like herself. She hoped he hadn't noticed, but it was impossible to speak in Penelope's tight, clipped tone all night.

'Mind if join you?'

Why the hell would Trent want to join Penelope on the beach? Emma thought they detested each other, yet here she was on the receiving end of some serious sexual chemistry. It was possibly one-sided, but from the way Trent's pulse thundered around the collar of his shirt, she didn't think so.

Emma's mind whirled. If Penelope and Trent were sleeping together, where did that leave her? If she avoided his advances, surely he'd get suspicious. If she went along for the ride, Penelope would undoubtedly find out and kill her. Not fire her, actually kill her.

She stood stiff, rooted to the ground. It was just a walk, and she could discover the truth about Trent and Penelope. They sure put on a great show of being enemies in public; it would be the perfect cover.

'All right,' she said before she could stop herself. Her pulse jumped in her neck. 'Some company would be lovely.'

THE NIGHT WAS warm and an almost full moon gave the beach a magical glow. Emma's body tingled as she grasped the hand Trent held out for her.

'Sit on that rock and I'll take your shoes off, otherwise you'll sink into the sand.'

He took her foot, cradling it in his hand as he undid the delicate ankle straps, one by one sliding her feet free from their constraints. Sitting opposite her, he pulled her foot into his lap. It was a simple movement, but she was acutely aware of how close her foot was to his crotch. Her toes froze, unwilling to accidentally brush over the firm bulge straining inside his trousers. Every nerve ending in her body vibrated with desire for him.

He helped her to her feet, but instead of walking, he pulled her against his chest. 'You know how long I've wanted this? Wanted *us* to happen?'

She'd dreamed about this. His words mirrored her thoughts, only they weren't meant for her. She tried to think of a suitable Penelope-ish reply, but instead she got lost in the spell his eyes cast. Wishing. Hoping. Praying that one day, by some miracle, the words could be for her.

He leaned in, dipping his head towards her and she let

her eyes flutter closed, preparing for the kiss. It was a kiss she'd imagined receiving a hundred times but never truly expected. From the first time she'd seen Trent, this had been her fantasy.

Her eyes sprung open and she pulled away from him. It was Penelope's fantasy, too, and Emma was stealing it. As much as she wanted him, tricking him into being with her wasn't the way to go about it.

'I'm sorry, I can't. I want to, believe me I do, but it wouldn't be right.' She fought to keep the emotion from her voice, but it bubbled up without permission.

'It sure feels right to me,' he whispered, running his hands over her arms, calming her, but at the same time, igniting a fire within.

'Me too,' she admitted as she fell once again under his spell. 'But it's not.'

His face fell. 'Are you worried about mixing business with pleasure?'

This could be the perfect excuse; she just needed to take it. But it wouldn't be the truth, and dishonesty had already made a mess of things tonight.

'No. It's not that. You don't know who I am.' She touched the mask, still firmly in place.

He took her face in his hands and pressed his forehead to hers. '*Yes*, I do.'

The way he gazed into her eyes, she almost believed it. Could he see it was her behind the disguise or did he think she was Penelope?

'No.' She pulled away and looked at the ground. 'You think you do, but you don't.'

He took hold of her mask and began to push it up towards the top of her head. 'Well, show me.'

Her hands snapped to the mask and held it firmly in place. If Trent found out about the boss swap and chose to get revenge on his business rival, he could alert the media. That would be worse than if Penelope hadn't turned up at all. She didn't want to think he'd do something like that, but he may feel betrayed when he found out her identity and the risk was too great.

'I can't.'

He smiled with kind eyes. 'Okay, but let's walk instead.'

They chatted as they strolled along, hand in hand. The more she got to know Trent, the more she liked him. It wasn't just a physical attraction anymore and the stakes had risen. They talked about their dreams and aspirations. She was surprised to find they had a lot in common, besides his social standing, of course. She wanted to work with children eventually, and the fact Trent was involved in a bunch of children's charities made her heart soar. They both loved reading, and he was currently making his way through a list of top one hundred books you should read before you die. She preferred romance novels and she couldn't help but draw comparisons between those books and what she was experiencing with Trent. They did agree on the classics though, and she found they had both studied literature at university.

They'd be so good together. She could just feel it. If only she could tell him who she was without risking Penelope's reputation and her own job. There had to be a way.

THE GROUND WAS STILL WET from the retreating tide. Time had slipped away from her and she couldn't help comparing her evening to that of Cinderella. Only difference was, Emma wouldn't get to keep her prince.

'What if I were to say I don't care who you are, I just

don't want this night to end?' Trent asked as if reading her mind.

She blinked up at him. 'Sort of like a one-night stand with a stranger?'

What was she saying? Was she seriously considering his proposal? This was her fantasy, but she worried she might be letting her lust for him lead her too far from reality by agreeing to something so bold.

'Sort of like that.' He pushed her hair off her shoulders, revealing her neck.

The desire she saw in his stare as he dipped his head, pinned her to the spot. Her feet sank deeper and deeper into the sand. If they sank much further, she'd be stepping all over her resolve.

She tried to think rationally, but the nibbled kisses he traced up her neck to her jaw prevented her from thinking of anything but him. She was in the moment and couldn't stop now, even if her life depended on it. She wanted him. All of him. If only for tonight.

'Deal.'

THE WORDS HAD BARELY LEFT her mouth when he claimed her lips with his, kissing her with an urgency that matched her own, as though he'd been the one watching *her*, dreaming about *her*, wanting *her*, instead of the other way around. His hands reached under her dress and slid beneath the elastic of her underwear, his fingertips teasing her flesh as he guided them down her legs.

Emma unzipped Trent's pants, tugging them loose and lowering them to the water pooling at their feet. He kicked them off and projected them towards their shoes discarded earlier. Any hope of being able to return to the masquerade ball vanished.

Undoing her dress, the muscles in his arms flexed with each button he worked. Running his fingers down her front, his hands gently brushed her breast through the flimsy fabric. He paused on the last button and she endured a torturous few seconds, waiting for him to glance at her. When he did, his eyebrow quirked with an unspoken question, but there was no way she was going to say no.

With a nod of her head, her erect nipples were freed as the dress fell smoothly from her body, rippling out across the water like a sheet of silver seaweed. He stepped out of his underwear, seemingly not caring what happened to it.

She stepped closer until their toes touched. But she wasn't satisfied. She needed him naked, completely, utterly, vulnerable. She'd imagined what he looked like under his shirt a thousand times and bit her lip in anticipation.

If this was her fantasy night with her fantasy man, she needed to see him—all of him. Even if she couldn't do the same for him and had to keep herself hidden behind the ridiculous mask.

She slid her hands under his shirt and splayed her fingers across his defined chest, tangling them in the short, thick hair. He removed a foil package from the shirt pocket and shrugged off the garment, removing their final barrier. It slid from his body, leaving him standing in all his naked beauty. For the briefest of moments, she thought her heart may have stopped beating and her eyes had forgotten how to blink.

She reached for him, but he dropped to his knees in the surf and gripped her arse. Drawing her to him, he parted her curls with his fingers and explored her folds with his tongue.

She took a sharp breath and held onto it, fearing he might stop if she moved. But she had no control over her primal moans and cried out into the darkness. Her heart raced as she lowered herself down harder against his mouth, rubbing herself against him until her legs shook. A wave of heat rolled within her, gaining momentum like a bubbling volcano threatening to explode.

Gripping his hair, she held him in place as her knees fought to clamp together.

'Oh, Trent!' She cried out as an orgasm ravished what was left of her shy-girl persona.

Trent lowered her onto the wet sand, the water immediately drawing a line around her before he pushed her legs apart with his knee so he could make her his.

The darkening of his eyes as he thrust into her told her he'd no time to tease her or ease her in gently and she was glad. She bucked against him, thirsty for more. She'd been building towards this in her mind for months, and the reality was better than anything she had imagined.

With each rhythmical motion, he grew bigger and harder and thrust deeper within her. His pelvis, as he slid in and out of her, ground against her bud, still swollen from just moments before. Her mind was a whirling euphoria and she fought to hold on, she wanted to reach her peak with him. She squeezed her eyes shut and tried to concentrate on the feel of his mouth exploring her body, nibbling kisses along her neck, trailing his lips down until they met her breasts. He sucked a nipple into the warmth of his mouth, making her arch her back. It was a tingling ecstasy like he'd flicked a switch and every nerve ending inside her came to life.

Her breath escaped her lungs in short, jagged gasps. She dug her fingers into the wet sand and squeezed them into fists, needing something real to hold onto. Something beyond the dream state she found herself in.

She was surfing on a wave, and as it rose to its peak, so did she for the second time in as many minutes. She cried out his name, begging him for release and as it crashed down all around her, she clung to him, the muscles in his back tense, rock-like as she gripped him. His body moved in unison with hers, their movements becoming one. The sheen on Trent's skin became a trickle and his thrusts sped until he groaned his release.

Rolls of pleasure continued to tumble through her and she had no energy to remove herself from the sea. She watched the deep rise and fall of his chest next to her and her racing pulse drummed along in time to his rhythm.

Lying in the shallows with water wrapping around her, the curves of her body fit perfectly with the broad planes of his. Like they were made for one another.

A blanket of stars covered them, the breeze, teasing the palm trees, serenaded them. A more perfect night had never existed.

'Tomorrow will be the first day of the rest of our lives. This is not a one-off, you hear me? I've been wanting you since the first moment I saw you and I won't settle for just tonight.'

Emma heard him, but her emotions waged war inside of her. Of course, she was happy to be here with him. To be kissing him and making love to him—*fucking him*—her brain corrected her. It was more than she'd ever expected and all she'd ever hoped. But there was sadness in the reality that, by tomorrow, he'd likely be with the real Penelope.

Was the pain she experienced and the hurt yet to come worth her one night with Trent?

Absolutely.

TRENT STRODE into the office the next day clutching a bunch of red roses. Every cell inside Emma's body snapped to high alert.

'Is Penelope in?' He barely even glanced at Emma. He was here for her boss.

Tears pricked her eyes and she swallowed back the lump forming in her throat.

'No,' Emma managed to croak out. She continued to stare at her laptop screen, mashing at the keys, a jumble of letters that made no sense but served to make her appear busy and unfazed by him. 'She's gone to the airport.'

'What's she doing there?'

'Business trip to Singapore. If you hurry, you might catch her.'

Why the hell had she said that? So Trent and Penelope could have their romantic airport moment and she could sit in the office mashing keys, pretending to think about anything other than the fact she was about to lose the man of her dreams?

He placed the flowers onto Emma's desk in front of her, and her fingers froze on the keys, but she dared not look at him.

'You really thought I could believe you were Penelope?' He shoved his hands in his pants pockets.

She dragged her eyes from the keyboard. 'You mean you didn't?'

'Not. For. A. Single. Second.'

She bit her lip to keep from laughing with utter joy. 'What gave me away?'

He rolled his eyes. 'Besides the fact you have the best arse I've ever seen and the clearest blue eyes, there are our conversations. You really think I could talk to Penelope about my desire to dig wells in Zimbabwe? She's about as deep as a kid's wading pool.'

'Don't forget our love of literature.' That was her favourite part of *them*, that she'd discovered she and Trent shared a love for the classics.

'Speaking of books, I hear Penelope's office has quite an extensive library.' He winked at her as he headed towards the private office.

Emma darted out from behind her desk and followed him. Once they were inside, she turned the lock and leaned against the door. He pounced on her like a puma with its prey, but she was his willing victim. He stooped, and his breath on her neck as he brought his lips down to kiss her had her body practically vibrating with desire. A rash of goose pimples spread down her arms.

As they clutched at each other, he spun them around and marched her backwards until she found herself pressed against Penelope's desk. His erection dug into her hip as she fumbled with his belt and zipper. He swiped his arm across the mahogany table, sending a shower of papers flying around her and lifted her onto the cool surface. When she freed his cock, it sprang to life and she gripped it, sliding her hand rhythmically over its length.

She increased her speed and tightened her grip, watching as he tilted his head back and let out a groan. A drip of moisture threatened to drop from its eye. She leaned in and ran her tongue around his knob until he grabbed her hair, pulling her back. Revelling in her ability to bring this powerful man to his knees, she smiled up at him and ran her tongue over her lips.

His eyes were locked with hers, neither willing to take their gaze off the other. Now that her mask had been removed and he knew who he was fucking, she didn't want him to look anywhere else but at her.

Little Gems

Want to try something a little sweeter?
Why not try our Little Gems Anthology?

Little Gems 2019:
Tiger's Eye

In 2020 we are refreshing the Little Gems to a new
anthology brand of Sweet Treats.

Think of all those yummy treats that make you feel good,
or that you might get or make for your loved ones.
The theme for 2020 is: CUPCAKES

All of the terms and conditions for Sweet Treats will
remain the same as they have been for Little Gems, with
full details found on the Romance Writers of Australia
website

https://romanceaustralia.com/contests-overview/sweet-
treats-anthology/

Previous Little Gems anthologies can be purchased from
the Romance Writers of Australia store
https://romanceaustralia.com/shop/

Fiona M Marsden

Fiona M Marsden started out as an avid reader. She was a late starter in finding romance novels, but once found, they became an addiction. It was only logical that the next step would be to write her own romances. She lives on a small rural property shared with families of kangaroos and wallabies, native birds, a koala and the odd possum, along with thousands of books, mostly romance.
Recent Release "Tell Me No Lies." 2019
Find her on Social Media as @FionaMMarsden or on FB as Fiona Marsden Writer. More about Fiona can be found on her website: http://www.fionamarsden.com.

Maisie Whitfield

Maisie Whitfield spends her work days at the keyboard writing media releases, website copy and rural fiction, but when the sun goes down, she pens sexy stories for readers who like it hot. Her rural lifestyle offers inspiration in droves, and she only has to look at the farmland out her office window to conjure up a new plotline. Normally a sauvignon blanc kind of girl, she has been known to drink whiskey and coke when Lee Kernaghan's buying. When she's not writing, Maisie likes to sew, avoid housework and read, read, read.

Kristin Silk

A long time student of human nature, Kristin Silk has loved writing from a young age. Although a late comer to romance writing, she has found her happy place in the world of happily ever afters. Kristin writes relationships based on respect and equality, with a dash of humour and a side order of sizzle. She is inspired by kindness, courage, love in all its forms, and people who bravely live their own truth. She resides in picturesque central Victoria with her husband, daughter and one very squeaky guinea pig.

Davina Stone

When Davina Stone isn't dreaming up hunky heroes and delectable heroines and plotting how to throw them together in pulse-racing sizzling scenarios, she can be found planting trees on her bush block, dodging snakes on long coastal hikes and learning to knit. Her goal is to complete the scarf she's been working on for the past two years and keep writing romances - the spicier the better. She regularly posts short stories at Davinastone.com and is a wee bit addicted to Instagram @davinastone_ where she would love you to join her for updates.

WL Davies

WL Davies began writing romances as a lark after leaving

her communications and editing job of many years. She enjoys cycling and makes good use of her amazing pedal-assist electric bike exploring the bike paths around her home. She makes her own jewellery and loves travelling and taking photos. Wendy won the Romance Writers of Australia Emerald Award in 2017 with her small-town contemporary romance, The Drover's Rest. The same story (renamed good enough for love prior to publication), was also a finalist in the 2017 Mid-American Romance Writer's Fiction from the Heartland competition.

You can catch up on her latest news via her Facebook page (https://www.facebook.com/wendy.davies.5688), on Goodreads (https://www.goodreads.com/wendyleedavies), or via her website (https://www.wendyleedavies.com). She loves hearing from readers, so don't be shy about dropping her an email (wendyleedavies2@gmail.com).

Josie Baker

Josie Baker lives, dreams and writes sensual romance, historical and contemporary. Share her sensual explorations at www.josiebaker.exposed, and read her collection of short stories 'Love, Lust & Nipple Clamps', available on Amazon. Josie is thrilled to announce the imminent arrival of six new steamy novellas, coming in 2019. Subscribe to her blog to find out when.

Suzie Jay

Suzie Jay is an Adelaide author who grew up within walking distance of the beach, dreaming of life as a famous author or Johnny Farnham's back up singer. After a

stint as a teacher and then a stay at home mum to six children, she decided to make her dream a reality. Writing romance, not singing, because she can't hold a tune and she's pretty sure she's tone deaf. Suzie didn't give up on Johnny all together though and in her spare time, she still sings along to 80's hits, bakes, and binges on Netflix with her own knight in shining armour- who's more likely to wear tattered footy jumpers than chain mail.
Connect with me:
Facebook (https://www.facebook.com/suziejayauthor/)
Twitter (https://twitter.com/suziejayauthor)
Website (http://suziejayauthor.com/)

Cassie Laelyn

Cassie Laelyn is a paranormal romance author who writes stories filled with love, loyalty and redemption. When she isn't daydreaming of sexy immortals, Cassie enjoys binging on TV shows, spending time with her family, and curling up listening to the rain. Cassie's debut paranormal romance novel, Unforsaken – Book one of The Fallen Guardians, is out now. You can find all the info on her website (www.cassielaelyn.com) , or you can stalk @cassielaelyn on Facebook, Instagram, BookBub and Goodreads.

Shannon Slique

Shannon Slique lives on the southern end of the Gold Coast in Queensland where she could spend her days drinking tea and watching the tides come and go – if only reality didn't intrude. She travels a lot with her husband

and that gives her insight into interesting locations for her
stories – both in Australia and overseas. Shannon loves
writing erotica, first because it deepens a romantic relationship between her characters and, then, just for the cheeky
naughtiness of it.

DM Inglis

DM Inglis has dabbled with writing for years, continually
promising to become more focused! Having not one but
two competition entries in different genres successful this
year has affirmed what friends and family have been telling
her for years; she can write. They have sworn to hold her
to account without reprieve until she delivers the goods
and completes some of her numerous manuscripts.

CL Rose

Books and reading have always been a big part of C.L
Rose's life. Married, she loves camp fires, cooking and red
wine not necessarily in that order. Keep an eye out for her
website, CL Rose Author, currently in construction phase.

www.ingramcontent.com/pod-product-compliance
Lightning Source LLC
Chambersburg PA
CBHW030424120726
47903CB00003B/796